JARED

Riverwise Private Security 3

ALISA WOODS

April 2019 Edition
Alisa Woods
Cover Design by Steven Novak

ISBN-13: 9781095657355

Jared (Riverwise Private Security 3)
Wolf Shifter Paranormal Romance

**He was broken by the war. Her secret could destroy her
family.** Ex-Marine sniper Jared River left the war, but the war
never really left him. He's a broken wolf who's only good for one
thing now—killing men. And he's peering down his scope at
Senator Krepky, the anti-shifter politician about to ruin the lives
of all the shifters Jared loves.

Grace Krepky is the daughter of the Senator, a good girl with a
passion for her father's politics and who's earned her way into
being his campaign manager. Only problem? She's secretly a
shifter… and the clock is ticking until her own father
inadvertently forces that secret into the open, ruining both their
lives.

Jared's all set to pull the trigger when he sees something shocking through the Senator's glass walls—his daughter is a wolf. Jared puts his gun aside to go after the fleeing girl, but he already knows this can only end in one of two ways—either he'll convince her to reveal herself to the Senator and stop his anti-shifter legislation, or Jared will have to assassinate her father.

If only she wasn't making him come alive again…

Chapter One

Jared had killed men before.

One more shouldn't make a difference.

He sighted down his scope, peering through the darkness at the tremendously lit-up house of Senator Krepky. The good Senator had a palatial estate on top of a mountain above Bellevue. It was beautiful—Jared could tell precisely how opulent the interior was because he could see *everything*. The exterior walls were mostly comprised of glass. The floor-to-vaulted-ceiling windows revealed the natural woods, polished granite surfaces, and sophisticated decor inside. With all that light blasting out, it was a good thing he'd brought his day scope and not just his night vision optics. But it was an easy target from his position across the ravine—he was lying on a bed of ferns under the drooping boughs of a pine tree with his M40A6 sniper rifle, complete with tripod mount and suppressor. Jared's skills were sufficient to achieve the kill, even at nearly a thousand meters to target. The 50mm bullet would not only travel the distance, punch through the plate-glass window, and vaporize the Senator's skull—it would finally bring Jared a kind of redemption. Or, if not that, at least an end to the meaningless days and tormented nights.

He wasn't a Marine anymore, and this wasn't Afghanistan: he would go to jail for this. And killing a sitting Senator? Death penalty for sure. Probably lethal injection, although Washington was the only state where hanging was still legal. But that didn't matter—he would find a way to die before he was locked up, waiting for his executioner.

One of the Senator's two personal security guards looped to the back of the estate, glancing over the expanse of lawn between the house and the forest. Jared flicked a glance at the guard, but the man just returned to the front. The wind gusted slightly, bringing up a fresh whiff of the creek at the bottom of the ravine. *Updraft.* About every three to five minutes. Avoiding that would keep his shot true.

Jared had been lying under his tree for an hour. The deed would have been done already, except the Senator was arguing with a young woman in his living room. She was a willowy, almost painfully thin girl, with long brown hair that fell in waves to her waist. Jared couldn't hear their argument, but whatever it was, the girl was giving the Senator hell. Jared stretched his leg muscles, relieving the cramping while still keeping his eye firmly on the target. He was really just watching them now—he had already decided the girl was the Senator's daughter, and Jared wouldn't kill him in front of her. It was one thing to hear the shot and find the body. She could choose not to look, if she wished. She might agonize about their last conversation being an argument—probably something pointless like the boys she was dating or the size of her trust fund or whether she could take out one of the five Jaguars the Senator kept on display out in front of the estate.

It was another thing entirely to watch her father's head explode.

Jared was a stone cold killer—he knew that, and there was nothing he could do to change the things he'd done in the service—but he sure as hell wasn't going to make a girl watch her father's brain splatter all over the living room. He knew the kind of nightmares that induced, the dead emptiness it settled deep in your bones, and he wouldn't wish that on anyone. Even the pampered princess of a senator who needed to die.

And Senator Krepky definitely needed to die.

The girl threw her hands in the air and turned on her heel. Jared held his breath, thinking she might leave, but she just whirled back again, having another go at the old man.

He let out the breath, slow and measured, just like he would when it came time to take the shot. He could wait. Waiting was all he did these days, one hollow day after another. The world kept buzzing around him, relentlessly moving on while he stood still.

And lately, all that activity had taken a turn for the dangerous. Shifters being kidnapped off the streets of Seattle. Assholes in the government conducting medical experiments. Men like Senator Krepky who didn't blink at the lives they wasted in pursuit of their wet dreams of power. Jared and his brothers, Jace and Jaxson, along with the rest of the River pack, had done what they could to stop it. They'd managed to liberate a ton of shifters from the horror show that was their government-sanctioned medical prison. In the process, Jace's mate, Piper, had discovered the Senator's plan for a new registration law for shifters... this was the same government that had already authorized medical experiments upon them.

It didn't take a genius to figure out where that was going. Not only would it be stupid-easy for the government to round up shifters, but shifter-owned companies like the private security firm Jared owned with his brothers, Riverwise, would go out of business. The public feared and hated shifters, which was why most stayed undercover, hidden just under the skin of Seattle. The military had discovered Jared was a shifter when he enlisted, but they kept that shit private precisely because they wanted shifter talent in the armed forces. And getting a job after the service would be next to impossible if they were outed as shifters. For most civilians, no one outside their family and their pack knew. And their lives would all be ruined by Senator Krepky's new law. Even proposing it would declare open season on shifters everywhere.

Jared wouldn't allow that to happen.

Krepky had to be stopped, and Jared was the only one for the job. His brothers had duties to tend to, a business to run—they weren't broken, like him.

And now they both had mates to care for, families to start. Things were good for them. Jared would be happy for his brothers, or possibly jealous, but his chest had been a dark cave of ice far too long for feelings like those. There was a reason he spent most of his time in the mountains or on the shooting range. He was only good for one thing now—killing. He could shoot anything, at any distance, under almost any conditions. He knew how to compensate for wind speed, direction, elevation, gravity, and spin of the damn planet. His shifter senses helped, but it was massive amounts of training that made him what he was. That, and a long list of confirmed kills.

But he wasn't a sniper for the Marines anymore. He'd done his job well, then walked away before he put the gun to his own head. At the time, that seemed sensible… but ever since he took that honorable discharge, he'd thought maybe that was a mistake. Maybe he should've stayed overseas until the war took him out. Easier that way. Better than walking around the streets of Seattle, surrounded by civilians living their ordinary lives, acting like he wasn't already dead inside.

Then this thing with the Senator came along. If Jared could stop Krepky from enacting a law that would destroy countless shifter lives… there wasn't even a question. It was the thing he had been waiting for—the reason he kept trudging on, day after day. He had something left to do, some purpose or reason why he was still alive, only he hadn't known what it was until he heard the Senator's plan. Then it became clear—this was for him to do and no one else.

Jared pulled in a deep breath of fresh mountain air, the pine scent calling to his wolf. The beast rose up under his skin and tuned his senses even tighter, sniffing the air and sensing the wind direction and speed. His eyesight sharpened as he peered through the scope once more.

It was entertaining to see the girl give shit to her father, but Jared knew his focus would wane with fatigue. Her finger-pointing and fist-clenching and red-faced fury needed to burn itself out soon, so he could get down to business and end the Senator's plans once and for all.

It only took a few more minutes of waiting to get his wish. The girl threw up her hands, turned on her heel, and this time, stormed away. She disappeared down the hallway for a moment, but then reappeared in what must be her bedroom, slamming the door. All the drama was exposed to him with those wide, glass windows. Speaking of people who lived in glass houses and the things they ought not do—the rock the Senator planned to throw at shifters was going to bring his glass house crashing down very soon.

The girl raged around in her room, and Jared took a moment to watch. She was delicate-boned and young—probably only twenty-five. Not really a girl anymore, but twenty-five felt insanely young compared to his nearly thirty-two. Of course, his mileage far outweighed his years. Her youthful, passionate anger took a long time to cool. In fact, it seemed to be going the opposite direction. She banged on the door and threw things around her room. He watched her for a minute longer, just to make sure she wasn't going to burst out of her room at precisely the wrong moment. But then something happened that made his mouth dropped open…

She shifted.

Jared squeezed his eyes shut momentarily, then yanked them back open. She was back to human, but there was no doubt she had shifted—because now she was buck naked. Small, high breasts. Delicate, narrow waist. Her abundant waves of hair covered her like a young Lady Godiva. Her fists

8

were still clenched, and her face was still red with fury.

Jared watched, transfixed, as she tugged her clothes back on at a furious pace. Then she bolted, straight out of her bedroom door.

He swung his scope back to the main room where her father was mixing himself something to drink.

She didn't appear.

Jared lifted his gaze and scanned the whole house, but he couldn't track her. He went back to the scope, but she was gone—vanished into some part of the house that wasn't visible from his position.

The Senator paced his living room, chugging whatever drink he had.

Jared should take the shot.

That's why he was here.

He lined up the sight and pulled in a steadying breath that also scented the air—the updraft was gone, the gusts were low. He could hear the soft whisper of the pines across the ravine, signaling the speed. He dialed the windage adjustment, let his breath out slow… and then grimaced as he pulled back from the scope.

The girl was a damn shifter!

The slow gears of his mind were winding up, cranked by that revelation—*the Senator's daughter*, for fuck's sake. What was that about? And where did she go?

A flicker of movement outside the house caught his attention. The guards were private security—Garrison Allied, one of Riverwise's competitors; Jared had checked out the company ahead of time, of course—but their patrols were all on the front side of the house where the winding driveway climbed the mountain to reach the estate. The back of the house opened up to the national forest, and that's where the movement was.

Jared swung his scope and scanned the darkened tree line—he caught sight of her just as she disappeared into the forest. Fully clothed. Running like the devil was on her tail. The Senator's daughter just… ran away.

What the hell?

The rest of the house was quiet. Her father was slamming back a second drink.

No one had noticed.

Jared gritted his teeth and tried to concentrate… but even before he lined up his scope again, he knew it was no use. His wolf was whining his ass off—Jared would have to go after her to make sure she was okay.

And *then* come back to kill her father.

Jesus, he was so fucked up.

He abandoned his rifle, leaving it set up under the tree, and shifted to his wolf form. The ravine between him and the house was long and deep. It would take forever to get through the underbrush as a man, but his wolf was strong and had four times the leap. He charged down the slope, using all his senses to navigate the complicated, dark terrain.

What the hell he was doing?

This wasn't the first time he'd had that kind of thought—sometimes he wondered if the frontal lobes of his brain were actually functioning anymore. He seemed to move on instinct more and more often. There were whole days he lost in the Olympic forest when he let his wolf take control, just as he was now. It was freeing—as if being *wolf* was a more innocent state. The sins he had committed were done by human hands. His wolf's paws hadn't pulled the trigger, again and again.

There were days when he thought he might go lone wolf. Never turn human again. Forget all the things that had happened, the mate he'd lost, the people he'd killed. But he knew that was just a fantasy. He could only be free of the nightmares in brief snatches when he was absorbed in work or exhausted by training. Or when he let his wolf run free like he was now, chasing after this girl.

This wolf daughter of the shifter-hating Senator.

It was hilarious and so fucked up. And it had derailed him completely. He shouldn't care about her—he should focus on the mission—but his wolf had latched onto her like she was suddenly everything that mattered in the world. Even the man in him couldn't just let her run off and get lost in the woods. *Or hurt.* He frowned with that thought and put more power into his stride up the far side of the ravine. He gave wide berth to the glass house and caught her scent not far into the forest bordering the Senator's house.

Then he stumbled upon her clothes.

She had shifted again, leaving her jeans and t-shirt just inside the edge of the forest, where they wouldn't be visible from the house. This girl had done this before, running off into the woods to be a wolf. Maybe. Her shift before had seemed... accidental. Maybe she had barely made it to the trees before losing control.

He scooped up her clothes in his mouth, which

made it difficult to pick up her scent. He was over-whelmed by the blueberries-and-cream mixed with angry-sweat smell that permeated them. He dropped her clothes again, padded away, found her scent-trail, retrieved the jeans and t-shirt, and charged off through the forest. He had to repeat that little routine a couple more times, but eventually, he broke out into a meadow in the moonlight. It was really just a small clearing, crowded at the edges by overgrowth from the forest, but it was open enough to easily see her prancing in the tall grass—not least because her wolf's brilliant white fur shone like a small moon had dropped down to play in the meadow. A light, growling sort of sound accompanied her dance. He couldn't decide if she was angry or just frustrated. Or maybe she was singing. It had a lyrical quality to it, almost like she was talking to herself. *In wolf.*

It was kind of adorable. Deep in his chest, a humming sound started, matching hers—like a growl but not quite—and his open mouth panted as he watched. His wolf was *reacting* to her in a way he didn't understand. He didn't reach out to her mentally, although that should've been possible—they were both in wolf form. Instead, he picked up her clothes, which had tumbled from his open mouth to the grass, and trotted toward her across the small field.

He could see the exact moment when she caught sight of him—her small wolf body jumped three feet in the air. When she landed, that white fur of hers puffed out and turned her into an extremely fuzzy version of the beautiful singing-and-dancing wolf from before. He slowed his pace. He was sure her growl was meant to be menacing, but it was about as threatening as a very small, very angry kitten.

Then he realized: she was terrified of him. And she should be. Meeting a strange wolf in the forest was dangerous for anyone, but especially a young female wolf. Some packs stole their mates, claiming the unmated females before they could be rescued. And unless the Senator *himself* was secretly a wolf, he doubted this girl had a pack—which left her even more vulnerable.

As he drew closer, her eyes went wide. They were a magical blue surrounded by all that white fur, making her seem almost otherworldly—an angel wolf, shining bright in the moonlight. But those beautiful eyes were zipping between him and the edge of the forest, as if she was contemplating making a run for it, but she was too terrified to move. The meadow grasses around her trembled with the breeze, but she was frozen.

He raised his head, hopefully showing that he was bringing her clothes, then dropped them in the grass a dozen feet from her. He yipped and backed away another dozen, finally planting his butt in the grass and waiting to see if she would take his offering.

There was a long stretch of seconds while she studied him, scenting the air.

He waited, still as a statue, but she didn't move. Maybe he would be less intimidating in human form? He shifted, still sitting in the grass. This took her by surprise, and she jolted again. But when he remained seated, she tremulously advanced toward her clothes, snatched them in her jaws, then backed away again.

He didn't move.

Once she was about twenty feet away, she shifted human. That glimpse he'd had before of her naked in her bedroom was on full display for him again—perky little breasts with nipples tightly puckered against the night's cool air; lithe body slender to the point of ridiculousness, but with a curvy little behind that made his cock sit up and pay attention; and that gorgeous hair, falling long all around her, almost hiding her nakedness. He felt like he should look away—he could see her furious blush even at this distance—but her hurried attempt to shove her clothes on kept him transfixed. Not to mention that his cock hadn't paid attention to anything in so long, he'd thought it was as dead as the rest of him. It made him feel strangely… *unbalanced.* As if he stood up, he might actually topple over.

Once her clothes were on, she asked, "Who are you?" Her bare feet crunched the grass as she backed away, clearly afraid of him.

Which she should be.

He stood up to talk to her, but his erection sprang out, and that suddenly embarrassed him. He covered it his hands clasped in front of him. That strange sense of unbalance threatened to actually tip him over, making the whole thing even more awkward.

"I'm not going to hurt you." His voice came out gruff, harsher than he wanted. He was a big man— he knew that—intimidating to most men, even shifters, not to mention girls whose waists were smaller than one of his thighs. It was the shifter gene, his time in the Marines, keeping in shape for his job at Riverwise—plus he'd been running himself to exhaustion with combat drills and training. They were the only things that let him sleep at night, but they also had the effect of keeping his body in top condition.

"How did you find me?" she asked, but she'd stopped looking for an escape at the edge of the forest.

"Followed you." Probably best not to mention he was about to kill her father before he followed her into the forest on a whim.

She narrowed her eyes. "Followed me from where? I came from my bedroom."

"I know. I was watching you." Well, that sounded pretty creepy. "I promise I'm not going to hurt you."

Her hands were wringing now, and a new look of anxiety blossomed on her face. "Are you... did my father hire you to watch me?" Her body was one big ball of tension.

He couldn't help it—he had to move closer to her. He took a couple, slow steps. "No, I promise. I don't work for your father. You have to know that's true—I'm a shifter." He let that hang in the air, because obviously *she* was a shifter, too.

Her eyes went wide, but her thin shoulders dropped, and her face relaxed. "You're from one of those shifters gangs my father's always talking about. You're spying on him."

"Something like that." He took another step toward her. She seemed less afraid of shifter gangs than her own father. *Interesting.* "I promise, I won't tell anyone your secret, including your father."

He could see the relief washing through her body, draining all the tension from it. "Thank you." The sincerity of it was so strong, so innocently grateful, even before she knew what he was all about… it *moved* something inside him. Something that wanted to *feel,* but the frozen cavern of his chest was hardened against any such thing.

"Why were you running?" He wanted to come closer, to reach out and touch her soft skin… but that was ridiculous. And besides, his hands were busy covering his junk—the idea being that he was trying *not* to freak her out and make her think he was some kind of predator.

She shook her head and darted a look at the edge of the forest again.

Shit. He was spooking her.

"Look, it's really not safe out here for you." He glanced around at the darkened trees. "I don't scent any other wolves at the moment, but we're in open territory. It's always possible someone could be lurking. And I'm assuming you're unmated."

"Unmated?" She wrinkled up her nose in a way that was painfully cute. "That's something you wolves do, right? Taking a mate? I mean, I've heard the stories."

"*You wolves?*" Jared frowned. "You don't know anything about us, do you?" *Of course.* She'd probably kept this secret her whole life. He wasn't sure how that was even possible, but she must have.

She looked pained. "I didn't mean... I just meant... I'm sorry." She bit her lip, and it was a good thing he was covering up his cock because it twitched when she did that. *Fuck.* What was that all about? It was like every little thing she did... he pushed that thought away and searched his memory for her name. He'd researched the Senator before coming to kill him, of course, but he couldn't recall it. She hadn't been important—not until she turned into a wolf.

And started giving him hard-ons without even trying. "My name's Jared. What yours?"

She laughed, a clear bell sound that rang of innocence. It left behind a smile that glowed in the moonlight. "You tracked me into the forest, but you don't know who I am? You're spying on my father, but you don't know my name?"

"I don't always do all my homework."

She let out a hiccupping laugh this time, bubbly and young-sounding, then she advanced toward him in light, quick strides, her hand outstretched to shake hands. "I'm Grace Elizabeth Dawn Krepky, daughter of Senator Timothy Krepky. Pleased to make your acquaintance, Mr. Jared Wolf."

His face heated—he would have to remove one of his hands from covering his privates in order to shake her hand. It was absurd that this embarrassed him, so he gritted his teeth and forced himself to do it. "Ms. Krepky."

She was sneaking looks at his barely covered erection, which only made it harder.

This was wrong. All of this was wrong. He shouldn't be talking to Grace Krepky, daughter of Senator Krepky. Jared shouldn't have followed her. He was going to kill her father, and here she stood, blushing at the hard-on she'd caused and worse… causing it in the first place.

She looked away, the red creeping up her cheeks obvious in the moonlight.

He cleared his throat. "I left my clothes… well,

back where I started. I'll shift and escort you back to the house."

She shook her head in amazement. "Why are you looking out for me?"

He just stared at her. He had no idea how to answer that question. "Just don't come out here by yourself anymore. It's not safe." Then he shifted before his nakedness could cause any more embarrassment for either of them. He turned to trot toward the estate, glancing to see if she was following.

He couldn't talk to her this way, which was better. Much better. But in wolf form, her blueberries-and-cream scent called even stronger to him. He loped ahead, putting distance between them, but taking the most human-friendly path through the underbrush and fallen pine trees. When they reached the edge of the forest near the back side of her house, he paused. No need to let the guards know a wolf had breached their perimeter.

Grace turned to him before she reached the edge. "Will I see you again? I have…" She clamped her teeth together, looking uncertain and glancing between him and the house. Then a look of resolution came across her face. "I have questions."

Would he see her again? No. Or at least… he

shouldn't. He wanted to shake his head or turn and disappear into the night, but instead, he found himself giving her a single dip of his snout. *Yes.*

Her answering smile was as natural on her face as sunshine. His wolf responded with an impulse to step forward and touch her, but he held it back. This was wrong—all of it was all kinds of wrong. The type of wrong that would end up with people hurt. And possibly dead.

But he stood still and did nothing that might diminish her smile.

She turned and snuck back to her house.

What in the name of magic was he doing?

Chapter Two

THE CAMPAIGN OFFICE BUZZED WITH ACTIVITY. Normally, the hum and bustle would electrify Grace, and she would be out in the thick of it, watching poll numbers, checking strategies, scanning news reports. But this morning her head was swimming, and she was hiding out in the tiny corner office she never used.

She had been caught.

Caught shifting. Caught running in wolf form through the national forest. Of all things, caught by a huge, gorgeous shifter who had stood before her in all his naked glory sporting a king-sized erection she could hardly keep from staring at. It wasn't like she had never seen a man naked before, although she could easily count the times, and none had involved a specimen like him. She had fantasized about him all night long.

Her vibrator had gotten a serious workout.

And he wasn't simply hot—he was jarringly gentle, unlike all the stories her father spouted about shifters. Never mind that *she* was a shifter, too —that was her dark secret, the one she kept from everyone. She certainly didn't *hang out* with shifters, and she only had second-hand knowledge of what they were truly like.

Until now.

Now her secret was in the hands of a man with only a first name—*Jared.* He had promised to keep her secret safe, but she had absolutely no reason to believe him. In fact, she had every reason to believe he would run to the nearest celebrity rag and spill the sordid details about the Senator's daughter who was a wolf.

She buried her head in her arms, which were folded on top of the scramble of papers on her desk.

This mystery shifter wasn't the only time bomb waiting to explode her life. Her father's new legislation to register shifters would destroy her just as fast. She'd argued endlessly with him about it, to no avail. It was like a vortex of bad luck was coalescing around her, threatening to consume her.

She should be finding a way to forestall the legislation.

She should be hunting for information on the mystery shifter.

She should be making plans to move to Bermuda.

But all she could think about was that scorching hot man standing naked in the moonlight. *Jared.* Even his name was sexy. And the size of him, with all those muscles and that huge cock… Jesus, were all shifter men that turbo-charged with masculinity? He had a military look about him, too, with the controlled movements and the clipped way he talked. Which only brought another flush of heat between her legs.

Would he return to the forest tonight? She couldn't help fantasizing about running out to meet him. He promised she would see him again—well, not exactly a promise. A simple nod from his dark, shaggy wolf form. One nod, and she was ready to run off and have sex in the woods with a man she barely knew.

An extremely hot man. *A shifter.*

God, her vibrator was going to need new batteries if he didn't show up tonight.

Grace groaned and dug her hands into her hair, bunching it up in frustration. Then she slammed her fists down on the papers on her desk, sending them fluttering. She had to get her mind off the hope of random sex with hot shifter men and focus on stopping the cataclysms from crashing down on her all at once.

She'd begged her father to put off the introduction of the shifter legislation—or to cancel it outright. Totally fallen on deaf ears, not that she expected any different. This anti-shifter registration law was going to be the cornerstone of his re-election campaign.

She should know—she was his campaign manager.

Normally, she was a true believer. Hell, she'd written most of his policies. And they seldom had disagreements when it came to her father's work. Together, they'd done a lot of good work— protecting the environment, looking out for the homeless. She was especially proud of his work on the behalf of veterans, those men and women who laid down their lives for their country. This shifter law was the first significant part of his platform that she'd even tried to talk him out of.

Obviously, it was a problem for her personally. Her father would disown her if he knew. His anti-shifter beliefs were true to the core. He had no idea his daughter was one, but she doubted that would make a difference. Which didn't just distress her and make her live in constant fear of discovery, for her sake and for his... it embarrassed her. She loved her father. He was a powerful man, and he used that power in good ways. He worked hard, and he truly cared about people. At least, that's what she had always believed. He wasn't racist or sexist or cling to any of the other bigotries and biases that often plagued men of his generation. He was a good man who believed in the goodness of people—the only problem being that he didn't seem to think shifters belonged in that class.

He called them animals.

He said they were dangerous.

And, the truth was, she couldn't really argue with that. Her beast had always felt like a wild part of her, one she had a hard time controlling. It was easy to believe that shifters—*other* shifters, the ones who let their animal side loose—could be a danger to others.

Only Jared hadn't done *anything* to hurt her. In fact, he'd watched over her, escorting her back to her house and making sure she was safe, even though she'd run through those woods a hundred times. Her father's idea of shifters seemed wildly at odds with the strong, silent man she'd seen in the meadow. Maybe that was why she was drawn to him… she pictured him naked again, and heat flushed through her lady parts.

No, it was definitely the raw, masculine hotness.

But her father's hatred of Jared's kind was real. Grace had been tempted, so many times, to tell her father what she was, but she had always held her back. Something about shifters repulsed him. Angered him. Maybe because he was such an alpha male himself, he couldn't stand the idea that men like Jared—physically superior with obvious sexual prowess, reeking of masculinity—were out there.

Maybe it was simple jealousy.

She didn't know why her father hated shifters quite so much, but all her entreaties to put off this legislation had been for nothing. In a week, he was sponsoring the bill.

One week. She had one week to figure this out. Then her days would be numbered.

She may have even less time than that, if this

hot shifter, now in possession of very valuable information he could use against her father, went public. The campaign manager part of her was already calculating all the ways to minimize the damage, but there was no escaping it—the PR would be devastating. She couldn't even wrap her head around what would happen to her, personally. If her mom were still alive, this would kill her.

She had one week to figure out how to avoid this Armageddon.

With interviews to schedule and a campaign kick-off tour to set up, she should just bury herself in work, like she usually did, and pray that an answer would come. Maybe the shifter in the woods would have an answer for her tonight. Or just a kiss. She would definitely settle for a kiss. More if he was willing.

Grace was shuffling through the paper disaster on her desk, trying to find her tablet, when her best friend and PR manager for the campaign, Kylie Anderson, burst into her office.

"All right, what are you hiding?" Kylie loomed over her desk, arms crossed, foot tapping impatiently.

Grace's heart lurched. "What do you mean?" *Jesus,* had the shifter already exposed her?

"You're hiding in your office, Grace. You're *never* in here. In fact, I was thinking about moving my crap in here and seeing how long it would take for you to notice. So what the hell is going on?"

Her best friend was short and roundish in a compact, sexy kind of way, with bouncy red curls and a personality the size of Montana. She took no nonsense from anyone, including Grace, yet could smooth-talk a Saudi Arabian prince out of oil rights. Grace had seen it happen.

But apparently, Grace's secret was still that. She sighed in relief, then tried to cover it.

Kylie just narrowed her eyes. "Grace Elizabeth, don't you dare try to hide something from me. How am I going to do my job if I don't know what's going on?"

She had a point. This PR nightmare would land squarely in Kylie's lap. Her best friend would loathe Grace at the level she reserved for polluters and child pornographers. And Grace normally told her every detail of everything... with this singular exception. Now she needed a lie to cover her current funk, and fast. Except Kylie could sniff out lies like bloodhound after a serial killer. So it needed to be damn close to the truth.

"I met a guy last night." Grace bit her lip

because Jared was hardly just *a guy* and thinking about him genuinely got her hot and flustered. Her wolf whined. "A really hot guy. Only I don't know if I'm going to see him again."

Kylie sprouted a grin as she hurried around the desk to sidle up to Grace. "What the... *when* did this happen? And why are you meeting guys without me? I thought we had a pact!"

Grace smirked. Neither of them had time for boyfriends—at least that was the excuse Grace gave every time it came up. Kylie was just as married to the campaign as she was. The truth was that Grace couldn't let herself get close to anyone—eventually, they would discover her secret. So she and Kylie had vowed that they were all about hot men and one night stands and that they would be each other's wing woman.

Only Grace never followed through—one night stands meant a very high risk of accidentally revealing herself. Then Jared came along and... he *already* knew her secret. There was nothing to lose.

"I kind of stumbled into him," Grace explained, hoping that would be close enough to the truth to convince Kylie. "And I can't get him out of my head."

"Hot?"

"Super hot. Like, burn out my vibrator hot."

"Yes!" Kylie fist-pumped on her behalf, and it made Grace grin. "So what's the problem?"

"Well… he's not really the sort I should hang out with."

Kylie's eyes lit up. "Oooh… a bad boy. *Yum.* Those practically set the bed on fire."

Kylie would know, but Grace certainly wouldn't. She was still a virgin, something she also kept from her friend, the sexual dynamo. Too hard to explain why. But maybe… with Jared…. Grace had considered it before. If she shifted while in the throes of passion with another shifter, there wouldn't be a need to explain. That was the real reason she had never gone all the way with a man before. Whenever she got riled—usually angry, but other passions could do it as well—her wolf threatened to come out. The beast within was hard for her to control under reasonably normal circumstances—and losing her virginity was not a normal circumstance.

Grace sighed. "I'm sure this guy would be insanely hot in bed."

Kylie shrugged. "So what's the problem? It's not like you have to marry him."

"I really can't even date him, Kylie." Grace bit her lip, hoping. "But you know what? Maybe I'll just come straight out and ask if he's interested. You know, just a one-night thing, then we go about our business." Maybe even *tonight,* she thought wistfully.

"Now you're talking. What guy is going to say no to *this?*" Kylie showcased Grace's slumped over form with her hands.

Grace straightened and glared at her.

Kylie retracted her hands. "Now that getting you laid is taken care of…"

Grace rolled her eyes.

"…we need to get back to work," Kylie continued without missing a beat. "I've got that photo op with the veterans at the VA hospital almost set up. Can the Senator be there this afternoon?"

Grace fumbled around for her pad, finally found it, and swiped it open, checking the calendar. "Looks like he's open from one to three. What's the story there?" It was a relief to talk about work again.

"Some outrage about the VA treatment of a veteran who came in, but they sent away."

Grace frowned. Their soldiers were ridiculously underpaid to begin with, and many of them had been to hell and back overseas—the least their country could do was give them decent health care. "Why did they send him away?"

"Something about how he couldn't fill out the registration forms properly. Some kind of mental confusion. Turns out the guy had diabetes and was going through an episode."

"How does something like that even happen?" Gracie stood up, her anger rising with her. "Tell them the Senator will *definitely* be there. I'll make sure of it. I'll work up some kind of policy statement in the meantime. Do we know who was responsible for turning the vet away?"

"Some new hire in the registration office," Kylie said. "Sounds like a training issue to me."

"New funds for training—got it." Grace made a note on her pad. "I'll look into it and get a statement together. Where's our speechwriter this morning?"

Kylie shoved away from the desk. "Nolan straggled in an hour ago. Not sure what his deal is—but I'd bet money he was out clubbing again last night." Kylie waved her fingers goodbye and strode toward the door of Grace's office. Just before she left, she grabbed the doorjamb and leaned back, stage whispering, "Speak of the Devil!"

Then she disappeared, and Nolan appeared in

her place, arms spread wide dramatically. "And he shall appear!"

Grace couldn't help but grin. Nolan was tall, lanky but well-built, with sparkling blue eyes that were usually filled with either humor or a smoldering sexiness that said he wanted to take her to bed. He had almost landed her, too. In fact, if there was ever a man Grace wished she *could* burn up the sheets with, it was Nolan Pearson. He was hot, smart, and had all the right politics. And had written many a fine speech for her father over the two years he'd been working in the campaign office. He'd almost talked her into taking the risk and crawling into his bed. Twice. And as he sauntered into her office now, she couldn't help wondering how she'd managed to say no. Other than the fact that it would unravel her life completely.

Which, it appeared, was just a matter of time, anyway.

But Kylie was right about him being out late— the dark circles under his eyes told a tale of club dancing and that scotch he liked. "Hard night picking up women?" Grace asked with a smirk.

He eased his hip onto her desk, glancing around with that same curious look that Kylie had, probably wondering why she was hiding out. Then his sparkling blue eyes found her again. "Grace Krepky, you know the only woman I want to pick up is you."

She waved away his standard flirtation, even though she knew it was true. "That doesn't seem to slow you down."

He leaned toward her, bracing his elbow on his knee to dip his head down. Definitely the bedroom eyes this time. "I'm just marking time, Gracie. All you have to do is say the word, and I'm yours." His voice was soft, and she knew he meant it.

He just didn't know it would never be possible. "We've got work to do, Nolan Pearson." She stood up, not least to move away from the temptation to do something she would regret. Especially when the agitation between her legs just seemed to keep growing.

He made a motion like she had just stabbed him in the heart, then staggered from his perch on the desk. "I am a serious glutton for punishment hanging around you, Grace Krepky. Someday, I'll wise up and go work for that other Senator. The one with the bad hair. I hear he has a *nice* daughter, one that won't torment me."

She smirked. "Someday you'll find a supermodel who's a policy wonk, settle down, have two kids, a minivan, and a hipster estate in Bellevue."

"Well, you don't have to be nasty about it," he said with a horrified look. "You could just say you find me terribly unattractive as a man. Or that you and Kylie have finally decided to consummate your lesbian love affair."

Gracie snorted, a totally ungracious sound, but that was one of the best things about Nolan—he made her laugh. "Well, both of those would be lies, and as the Senator's daughter, I'm sworn, at all times, to tell the absolute, complete, and total truth."

He mock-scowled at her. "You need to work on your skullduggery skills if you want to be a proper politician's daughter." But she could tell she was forgiven. For now.

"Back on task, Pearson," she said with her best drill sergeant voice. "I need you to write something up for the Senator to say at the VA hospital today."

"We're doing that? *Excellent.* Saw that on the news. Whole thing royally pissed me off."

Grace smiled—Nolan really was just the right kind of guy she could settle down with. As if settling down would ever be in the cards for her. But he was sweet and passionate about all the things she cared about, unlike the grim, dark, and brooding shifter in the forest. Jared didn't even crack a smile the whole time. It was sexy as all hell, she had to admit. Maybe, if she got lucky, she could stamp her V-card and convince him not to spill her secret, all at the same time. If she could somehow mash together sweet and charming Nolan with a brooding and sexy shifter like Jared, they would make the perfect man for her.

But there would never be a perfect man for her. She knew that already.

Grace kept her smile bright for Nolan. "I'll have some policy details for your speech in an hour or so."

Nolan nodded. "Perfect. I'll sketch up a skeleton speech for now, and we can plug in the details later." He made for the door, then paused at the threshold, turning back to her. "There's a new Belltown wine bar I was looking to try out. Want to be my arm candy?" He gave her a small, tenuous smile. The kind that came with promises she had a hard time saying no to.

"I'm booked up for life," she said with a resolute nod. "But if this week doesn't look up, I might need some libations at the end of it to get me through."

He frowned and stepped back into her office. "Something wrong?"

"No," she said quickly. She shouldn't have said anything. "Nothing I want to talk about." A small flame of hope burned in her that maybe, someday, she could share everything with a man like Nolan. Today was definitely not that day.

He nodded and hesitated before turning back to the door. "Just say the word, Gracie." Then he took his sexy half-grin with him, and Grace fell back into her chair.

She should bury herself in creating a policy statement about VA hospital funding improvements... and worry about Nolan and the hot shifter guy, Jared, later. All of that was moot anyway. Her real problem was the fact that she was the shifter daughter of an anti-shifter politician, and that fact was going to come out soon.

Very soon.

Chapter Three

"You were going to *what?*" That was Jaxson, Jared's younger brother.

"What the actual fuck, Jared?" Jace, his youngest brother, was well and truly pissed.

"You can't just assassinate a sitting Senator!" Jaxson acted as though this would never occur to him—which it probably wouldn't. He was a good man.

"You were—" Jace gestured to him with inarticulate rage, then turned to Jaxson. "He was trying to get himself killed."

"I was trying to get Senator Krepky killed," Jared clarified. What happened to him didn't matter so much… and, for the record, he didn't actually have a death wish. You had to be alive to want to die, and Jared hadn't had a spark of anything he'd call *life* for a long time. Except for that moment in the meadow…

Jaxson was reduced to running his hands through his hair and cursing under his breath. Except for the three of them, hovering in the kitchen, everyone in the safehouse was still sleeping, even though dawn had broken hours ago. But Jared could hear rustlings—some of the many shifters who called the River family estate their temporary home were starting to stir. Soft footfalls sounded on the stairs, but his brothers didn't seem to notice. Too busy having some kind of silent conversation between themselves that they thought he couldn't interpret. But he knew them too well—he'd knew what their reactions would be long before they had them.

It was just that none of it mattered. He would do what needed to be done.

Piper—Jace's newly-claimed mate—padded into the kitchen, barefoot and rosy with the sex she'd no doubt been having with his brother all night. Jace and Jaxson stilled their frantic gestures at the sight of her. She screeched to a halt with her bare feet just inside the kitchen door.

"Okay," she said, drawing the word out.

"Somebody want to tell me why it's Defcon1 in here?" She looked warily between each of the three of them.

Jared liked Piper.

Jace gestured angrily at him. "My idiot brother almost shot Senator Krepky last night."

Piper gave him a slightly impressed look, then a small nod to her mate. Jared almost smiled, but he didn't do that sort of thing anymore. He wasn't sure his face still knew how.

But now he liked Piper even more.

"*What?*" Jace's face turned even more red. "You *knew* about this?" He threw the accusation at Piper.

Hang on. Jared didn't want to make trouble between the new mates, although truth be told, Piper and Jace seemed to make trouble on their own just fine.

Before he could come to her defense, she spoke up. "Did I *know?* As in, do I pay attention to what's going on around here and have some clue about your brother's death wish? Yes." She gave a hard look to Jace, then Jaxson, both of whom were rubbing the backs of their necks and looking uncomfortable. And not looking at him.

But Piper did. "So what stopped you?"

"A girl."

Her eyebrows raised. "Well." She said it like the word was full of meaning. "That's interesting."

"It's not like that," Jared said. Only it was. Maybe. He couldn't decide why, and he sure as hell couldn't put it into words, but Grace had reached across that ravine and touched him in some way that was still stirring things around inside him. Things that hadn't been stirred in a long time.

"If it's not like *that*," Piper said, "then how is it?"

"She's a shifter." Jared took in the surprised looks on their faces, one at a time. He knew what they were thinking, and he'd had a couple more hours to think about it. Plus he'd finally researched Grace—not to mention talked to her and got naked with her in a field in the middle of the forest. That image of her, first wolf then bare-skinned human… his mind kept conjuring it in an endless loop. Far more often than he would've guessed, even as pretty as she was in both forms.

"The Senator's daughter is a shifter." Jace said it with an open look of surprise that seemed stuck on his face.

"She's kept it a secret." Jared eased up from his chair, working the stiffness from his muscles. He had hauled ass back for his rifle, just in case the girl had decided to turn him in after all. But she hadn't. Once he was there, he could have pulled the trigger—the Senator was still in the living room, none the wiser—but he didn't. Because now there was a chance of a better way.

"How do you know she's kept it a secret?" Jaxson asked, a shocked look still on his face. "In fact, how do you even know she's a shifter?"

"I saw her shift. She told me about the secret part, although I had already guessed it—can't see how she would share that with her father."

"She must not have any idea what he's up to," Piper said with a frown. "I mean, come on. If she knew her father was experimenting on shifters…"

Jared turned to her. "We don't know what she knows, not for sure. But we don't have to. We know the Senator wants to implement the registration law—that's enough. And I'm pretty sure she knows about that."

Jaxson's face went from shocked to puzzled. "What makes you think she knows?"

"She's his campaign manager." Jared would've known that earlier had he actually done his homework.

"Oh man." Jace's eyes were bugging out, but the surprise was back for all of them. And it *was* a hell of a thing. He thought maybe that was what stirred his insides—part of him wanted to dig her out of this hole she was in. Rescue her. Because she seemed stuck in an impossible situation.

"Blackmail. That's the answer." Piper was the one who said it, but Jared could tell they were all thinking it.

"No." He wasn't going to let that happen.

"You were going to kill her father—" Jace this time.

"And I still might."

That brought them all to a screeching mental stop.

"Jared, no—" Jace was shaking his head furiously.

"I will if I have to. I'd like to see you try to stop me, bro." He softened his tone a little. "This is my thing to do, not any of yours. You have lives, ones I'd like to protect. I'm the one with nothing to lose here."

Jaxson looked like he wanted to rip out Jared's liver for speaking the truth out loud, but instead he shuffled over and laid a heavy hand on Jared's shoulder. "I told you, no more of this lone wolf crap."

Jared shook his head. "That doesn't change anything. But *she* might—the daughter."

Jaxson frowned. "What do you mean?"

"I want to get close to her." At Piper's raised eyebrows, he added, "Yeah, okay, she *is* a beautiful woman, and any man would want to get close to her that way. But that's not what I mean."

Her eyebrows stayed raised, and she added a smirk in Jace's direction, but his brother was still shaking his head. "Is this really about *the girl?*"

"Yes. And no. She may not realize it, but she's in the same boat as the rest of us. Plus she has no pack, an asshole for a father, and no one she can depend on for help. I just want a chance to convince her of those facts."

Jace's eyebrows raised, but this time he was nodding. "So… exactly how do you propose to get close?"

"And what are you going to do once you're there?" The suspicion was obvious in Jaxson's voice.

But Jared would be a straight-shooter on this, just he was on everything else. He only lied when he had to. "I want to pose as her bodyguard. Spend time with her. She doesn't know anything about the shifter world, and she *needs* to… if she's going to have any chance of convincing her father to stop the bill." He took a deep breath, not at all sure it would work. "If she can't stop him, I will."

Jace shook his head. "Jared, for God's sake——"

"I'm not saying it's going to work. But if I'm going to give it a try, I'll need your help."

"Olivia's got a whole lot of materials to take to the press," Jaxson offered. "There's stuff in there implicating the Senator. We might be able to take him down that way."

"I know what you've got, Jaxson. An envelope? That's nothing—nowhere near enough to tie the Senator to the experiments. And you'll just give him a heads up… and time to weasel out of it. He's a politician. He'll probably flip it to his advantage somehow. Can't give him that chance. I need you to hold Olivia off, give me time to work on Grace."

"Grace? Is that her name?" Piper asked, dashing a look to Jace. He frowned in return.

"Grace Elizabeth Dawn Krepky. That's how she introduced herself."

"Had quite a little chat, did you?" Piper's eyes were shrewdly examining him, while at the same time, they held some kind of ill-defined humor. He wasn't quite sure why she was having a laugh at his expense, but it didn't bother him. Nothing did, not really. None of this was important. They could quibble over details, and he really could use their cooperation, but when it came down to it, only one thing mattered—stopping the Senator. If Jared was lucky, he'd find a way to save the Senator's daughter along the way.

"She trusts me, I think," Jared said to Piper.

"Why?" Jace asked. "I take it she doesn't know you tried to kill her father."

"She trusts me because I could have killed *her*, and I didn't. Plus I have her secret now." He still remembered her standing there, defenseless in the middle of the meadow, afraid of him but not running. Brave and innocent and beautiful. That was part of it, too—those things had stirred something inside him. Then she decided he was okay enough to come shake hands. It was a smart move, actually. Disarmed him completely and put him off his balance. Not that putting him off his balance was hard to do. Keeping tethered to reality was the hard part.

Besides, he promised he would see her again. He would hold up that much at least.

"Okay, how are we going to do this?" Jaxson asked. "Off the top of my head, I'm not seeing how you can get close enough to the Senator's daughter to shout hello. Unless you're planning on breaking and entering?"

"Garrison Allied does private security for the Senator's estate." This part Jared had already worked out on his own. "They owe us a couple favors. We tell them we have some intel that the daughter is messed up with the wrong kind of crowd. Say it involves one of our clients, and we'd like to put a bodyguard on her. Firstly, ensure her safety. Secondly, to get some intel for our client. We'll say we've got credible evidence she's under a specific threat as well, something that will convince the Senator that his daughter needs a bodyguard. That's me. I work the daughter, trying to convince her to come to our side, to understand where her best interests lie in all this. Failing that, I get some inside knowledge on the Senator himself that might implicate him and take him down for good. Failing that, I'll look for an opportunity to carry out my original mission."

"Putting a bullet in his head." Piper's voice was flat. "There are still other options you haven't considered, Jared. I can get into the Senator's office as well." Her counterintelligence experience had uncovered the Senator's plans to begin with.

"All right, then." He gave her a nod. "You work that angle, while I work mine."

Jace was still shaking his head. "We've still got *several* options before you put that last one in play… as if that's even an option. *Which it's not.* Like Olivia going to the press. Or blackmail—I like that option. *A lot.* If you can't get the daughter to come on board, then I say we put the pressure on to force her."

Jared nodded, although he had no intention of letting his brothers blackmail Grace. She was an innocent in all of this—that much he was sure of. And he wasn't going to let anyone ruin her life by outing her as a shifter. That was what he was trying to prevent—and if anyone was going to be sacrificed to the cause, it was going to be her asshole father. And Jared himself on death row. Grace would come out of this untouched if he had anything to do with it. He would fight his brothers to make that happen—because it was right, and they knew it, even if they were overly concerned about his life hanging in the balance.

"Lean on Garrison Allied to get me in," Jared said. "Give me a week to work the daughter. After that, we'll consider your other options." Of course, what he really meant was that *they* could consider their options while *he* was considering the best angle to snipe the Senator.

"I'll do what I can to find out if a week is enough time," Piper put in. "I'm not sure what the Senator's timetable is, but I think I can find out."

Jared gave her a sharp nod, and he felt sure that she understood—there were really only two options in his mind.

Either he'd convince Grace to help them, or her father would have to die.

Chapter Four

GRACE'S SMALL, RED FIAT CLIMBED THE HILL TO THE estate.

All things considered—including the fact that her life was going to implode within a week—the afternoon had gone well. The photo-op at the VA hospital couldn't have been any more moving or perfectly pitched as PR. It was the best possible warm-up for next week's launch of her father's re-election campaign. Nolan did an outstanding job with the speech, per usual, and Kylie made sure all the right members of the press covered it—she even managed to include the veteran who was turned away. Grace hoped her ideas about new onboarding requirements for VA staff—lining them up with the best practices of top-rated hospitals—would gain some traction in the Senate. In truth, the administration could implement them right away, if they chose to—sometimes, it just took the right political pressure at the right time with the right photo-op to get the bureaucrats to do their job.

That was what Grace loved about her work—making real things happen for real people. This kind of change, if it went through, could affect so many people's lives every day. During the photo-op itself, Grace's father was his usual stately self, delivering Nolan's speech as if the words had naturally come to him on the spot. Grace may not agree with her father about his new shifter legislation, but there was no denying he was an accomplished politician who could make things happen. After the photo-op, he had returned home, while she went back to the office to tie up loose ends and plan the calendar for the next day. Things would just get more frenetic the closer they got to the campaign launch.

The sun was sinking in the West, and its rosy hue turned the soaring pine trees surrounding her home into a mystical forest. As she pulled into the long winding driveway, she couldn't help thinking about the sexy shifter she met last night—and wondering if he would be returning tonight.

God, she hoped so.

Whenever she thought of him, it was an instant fully-body turn on. She'd never felt anything like it, even with smart and sexy Nolan-the-speechwriter. She couldn't tell if she was just desperate for sexual release or if the intense attraction was simply a natural response to the devastating sexiness of the man. Were all shifters that way? Or was it just him?

She parked her car in the vast garage where her father kept his showpiece vehicles. Her Fiat was plain-looking next to all the Jaguars, like a poor cousin who had come to visit, but she didn't mind. Sometimes she felt like the one normalizing force in her father's life—the thing that connected him to the real world where people didn't live in mansions and drive fancy imports. Even though, truthfully, she did both of those things, too.

She strolled toward the front of the house and gave a smile to Richard, one of her father's private security guards. Security was a constant presence around the estate, ever since she was a kid and her father was first elected to the Senate. To her knowledge, there hadn't ever been a real threat to their safety, but her father had always said the price of being a public figure was the loss of a certain amount of privacy. The guards were always professional and practically invisible most of the time. She didn't give them much thought, other than to politely acknowledge their presence. To do otherwise—to completely ignore them, as her father did —always felt a little wrong to her. They rotated a lot, so it wasn't like she got to know them personally, but they were still human beings, doing their job— and doing it well, as far she could tell.

"Good evening, Ms. Krepky," Richard said. He was a tall, broad-shouldered man, and he made her feel more secure just having him around.

She grinned. "All quiet on the Western front?"

"Everything's secure," he replied with a small smile. "I'll leave it to you to decide the rest, Ma'am. Your father requested that you visit him in his office when you arrive."

She frowned, but she knew better than to ask for more details, and just strode through the door Richard held open for her. The wide entryway was empty, not that she expected to see anyone. The house was lightly staffed these days, with just a housekeeper and cook as well as a gardener who only came on the weekends. Her heels clacked on the marble flooring, and she smoothed back her wayward hair as she wound through the halls to her father's office.

One of Grace's fondest memories was brushing

her mother's long hair at night, pretending she was Rapunzel and Grace was rescuing her from the castle by twisting it into a long braid. When the cancer struck, the first thing to go was her mother's gorgeous brown locks. Grace felt like her world was shattering with each clump she found abandoned on the floor. The chemo treatments were useless, and the cancer took her mother quickly. That was ten years ago. At the time, Grace didn't know if she would survive. But ever since, Grace had grown her hair out, long and straight and all the way to her waist, just like her mother's, with only the occasional trim to keep it neat.

It reminded Grace of her mother every day, but it annoyed her father to no end. He had ideas about the proper, professional length of a woman's hair, and Grace pretty much blew that out of the water. She tried to keep it under control in his presence, so she bound it up with a small band that she kept in her pocket just for that purpose. She was an expert by now, and in just a few seconds, it was restrained in a knot that tucked neatly at the nape of her neck.

She checked herself in the mirror outside her father's office, and it looked decent enough.

She knocked on the thick wood-carved door, then entered without waiting for a response. Her forward momentum came to a screeching halt, hand frozen on the doorknob when she saw who was inside.

Jared.

She gaped—her father was standing next to the shifter, speaking in calm tones. A buzzing sound filled in Grace's head, and a hundred thoughts ran through her mind, but they all settled down to one thing—*Jared was a spy for her father.*

Her world was about to crash down around her ears.

She almost turned and fled—the only thing stopping her was the fact that her knees were locked, and her hand gripped the doorknob so hard, she wasn't sure she could like go.

"Grace." Her father beckoned her over. "I'm glad you're here. I have something to discuss with you."

She made a horrible squeaking sound, deep in her throat. Jared finally turned to look at her with cool, calculating eyes. He was even more gorgeous in his dark tailored suit and polished black shoes than he had been the night before in all his nakedness... but the look in his deep brown eyes was inscrutable.

There was no running away from this.

With great effort, she forced herself into the room, one awkward step at a time. She almost forgot to let go of the doorknob.

Say nothing. Admit to nothing. Don't tip your hand.

Her mind was reeling, but she managed to reach her father's enormous desk, where Jared and her father were standing, without passing out.

"I know you like your independence, Grace," her father said, calmly, "but I hope you'll consider this with an open mind."

Grace stared at Jared. He held her gaze, unblinking. No smile. No emotion. Nothing to give away what was going on.

She forced herself to drag her gaze to her father. "Consider what with an open mind?" Her heart was pounding so loud, she was afraid they both could hear it.

Her father sighed. "I'm going to make my announcement for re-election soon, and you know that's going to be a somewhat contentious announcement."

Contentious. As in, extremely controversial. The shifter legislation was designed to be exactly that—a call to arms about the shifter menace among them, and the determined Senator who was going to do something about it. They had been arguing last night about it, but it was supposed to still be top-secret—had he told this shifter about it? Something wasn't right here.

"As we discussed before, it's not too late to change course with that," she said cautiously. What was going on here? Did her father know she was a shifter, or not?

Jared didn't move a muscle, but his eyes lit up at her words. He couldn't possibly know what they were talking about—could he?

Her father cleared his throat. Only she would be able to detect the disapproval in that small noise, but it was there. Only it was nothing like the level of raging disapproval, not to mention stunned anger, which would come if he knew what she was.

"And as I said, it's the key part of the platform." Disapproval that she'd brought it up; also a touch of impatience. "And I have even more plans beyond that as well." A warning. "But there are some risks inherent in this course of action. Ones I hadn't fully considered."

Grace narrowed her eyes—what was her father talking about? "I don't think we should—"

He cut her off with a raised hand. "I'm not

talking about political risks. I'm willing to take those —that's what a good leader does, taking the risk to do what's right. What the people need, even if sometimes they don't always understand that. Although some certainly do. No, Grace, I'm talking about the kind of risk I really don't like to take."

Grace's head was still swimming. *He doesn't know.* He wouldn't be standing calmly in his office if he did. He'd be throwing a fit or throwing books or throwing her out.

Play it cool. Figure this out. "What kind of risks are those?"

"The kind that threaten my family." He gestured to Jared. "I think it's best that you have a personal bodyguard from here on out. At least through the campaign."

Her eyes widened, and her heart climbed into her throat. "Bodyguard?" Her eyes flicked to Jared —again with the inscrutable face, but she detected a hint of humor in his eyes. A tiny crinkling around the edges.

Her father folded his arms, as if he was expecting a fight from her on this. "This is Jared Bachman. He's one of Garrison Allied's top personal bodyguards. They've heard some chatter on the street, especially among the shifter gangs, that hinted you might be a personal target. A way to get at me. I don't know how they know about the legislation, but it's obviously already leaked in some capacity. And they see you as my soft underbelly. I don't want you endangered in any way, Grace." He took a breath. For patience. *"Please.* I know it will be inconvenient, and I know you're against this in the first place, but I'm moving forward regardless. And I'd feel much better if I knew you were protected at all times."

Grace's mouth hung open. She struggled for words, but they simply wouldn't come. The crinkles around Jared's eyes deepened. He was laughing at her, on the inside, she would bet her life on it.

She turned to stare him straight in the face. "I guess I can tolerate a bodyguard for a while." It took everything she had not to give any indication that she knew he was much more, or perhaps less, than a bodyguard of any kind.

What in the world was he up to? And how had he managed to do this? Her head was whirling again, but this time with an unabashed excitement, not fear. Jared hadn't blown her cover. He'd kept her secret. What's more—somehow, he had managed to find a way to see her again. Not just once, but an ongoing, 24/7 personal bodyguard.

This was like a very naughty fantasy come true.

Her nether parts were already heating up.

Unbelievable.

Her father clasped his hands together. "Wonderful." Then he reached to hold her by the shoulders, something he never did. She couldn't remember the last time her father had hugged her. She almost forgot to hug him back, and only barely managed it before he quickly released her.

"Thank you, Grace," he said quietly. "It means a lot to me, your support in this. I don't want to have to worry about you."

Her father didn't need her support, at least not emotionally. Or in any other way, really. Of course, she supported him tremendously in being his campaign manager, but that was just a given. Doing her job. Part of Senator Krepky's vast empire that he used to effect his political goals. There were some privileges in being his daughter—she got a pass on things he'd fired mere employees for—but she knew the bodyguard just meant one less thing distracting him, so he could focus on the campaign. Which was fine.

Even better—her cataclysm had been averted for the moment.

Jared finally spoke up, extending his hand. "A pleasure to meet you, Ms. Krepky." The smiling lines had disappeared from his eyes. Now they were smoldering hot sexiness at her. Or maybe that was just her imagination, sparked by the heat of his hand on hers. It was like an electric shock had bridged the space between them and enlivened her entire body.

"Mr. Bachman." She dipped her head and hoped the heat in her face wasn't turning it beet red. Her father had already moved on to attend to some business on his phone.

"Please, call me Jared." He was holding her gaze so intensely, her mouth went dry. They needed to be alone. To talk. *Now.*

"Well, Jared, I have a few things to do yet tonight. I suppose you will be accompanying me?"

He tipped his head in acknowledgment. "I'll try to be as unobtrusive as possible. And I'll make every effort to respect your privacy, Ma'am." He was telling her something—that he was still keeping her secret. Perhaps.

"If you call me *Ma'am,* you'll just summon the gray hairs to my head at a faster clip. Please, call me

Grace." She was saying this primarily for her father's benefit, but he wasn't even listening. Grace stepped back and beckoned Jared with her head. To her father she said, "Great photo-op today, Senator. Tomorrow's schedule is full as well."

Her father made a noncommittal nod, waving her off as he attended to his phone.

She had been dismissed.

She gave a wide-eyed look of *What the hell is going on?* to Jared, then turned on her heel, expecting him to follow.

As she strode toward her bedroom, she licked her lips in anticipation. The other security guards generally stayed outside, toward the front—she knew this from the many times she'd slipped out to the forest when her wolf was raging under her skin, wanting to get out. But since Jared was her *personal* bodyguard, she figured that meant bringing him into her bedroom was entirely appropriate. Hot as sin, but completely excusable, if they were caught.

A tight, low, and giddy feeling danced in her stomach. Was this really happening? She didn't look at him or say anything until they were alone with her door closed.

She whirled on him. *"Oh. My. God.* Do you want to explain this?"

He just stared at her for a moment, then said, "I made you a promise."

What kind of explanation was that? She threw out her hands in exasperation. "My bodyguard? Seriously? Do I even want to know how you pulled that off?"

"Probably not." The small lines were back around his eyes, but it wasn't a true smile. He was like a wall—tall, dark, sexy, and... *closed*.

She couldn't make sense of him at all. "Why are you here? Tell me the truth. And by the way, thanks for not spilling my secret. Then again, I guess I could've spilled yours as well." His inscrutableness was making her testy. That, and the raw voltage sexual tension that had her ready to climb out of her skin. Or climb over his. Or something.

This much she knew: Jared was a spy of some kind. She just didn't know what kind.

"You said you had some questions." He dipped his head to peer into her eyes. "I'm here to answer them."

She gave him a skeptical look. *"That's it?* Come on, I'm not an idiot. I know you're spying on my father." Did he know about the legislation? Was that what this was really about? "And what was that business about the shifter gangs threatening me?"

"Cover story. It's what I had to do to get here. To be with you."

"With me?" Her heart was lurching around inside her chest. "And why would you want to do that?"

His face softened in a way that was hard to describe—like he felt sorry for her. Or perhaps he heard the tremble in her voice.

He took a step closer and dropped his voice. "You don't know anything about being a wolf. You have been trapped here, living a lie, probably your entire life. There are things you need to know. I'm here to teach you."

His soft, deep voice, his towering form, all muscular and male—all of it was insanely heating every corner of her body. "What things are you going to teach me?" She could hear the breathy neediness in her voice. *God,* she was desperate. Pathetic, really. But here was a man who was sexiness personified, in her bedroom, offering to *teach her things.* Any woman with a pulse would be hoping those things would be happening in her bed.

"What do you want to learn?" The deep timbre of his voice was going straight to her lady parts.

Oh my God. "I'm… I'm really new to all of this."

She was going to combust if she had to speak anymore.

"Then we should get started right away." He stepped back and swept his hand to the door, waiting and giving her an expectant look. "How about we go for a run?"

A shiver ran through her that was almost more than she could take.

Chapter Five

THE SCENT OF GRACE'S AROUSAL WAS MAKING HIS body tight.

He had that unbalanced feeling again. It had been so long since he had felt anything like the deep churning in the pit of his stomach that she caused. Since he had felt *anything* at all, really. And this was more than simple lust, although there was plenty of that… it was a melting of sorts, like he was coming out of a deep freeze and into the sun for the first time. Only the freeze was the only thing that held him together. She didn't have to do anything, or say anything, in particular—just her nearness made him feel like he was coming apart at the seams. But her obvious need, the scent of her arousal, was amplifying it a hundredfold, telegraphing straight to his wolf a message that kept repeating—*take me, take me, take me.*

As if she could ever belong to him.

They had snuck out the back of her house and were now running across the open field toward the forest. He was right—she done this before. She knew exactly which path to carve across the tightly trimmed lawn to avoid the security cameras and the line-of-sight of the guards patrolling the front. She kept throwing little grins back at him that threatened to melt him a little more. He could've followed her with his eyes closed—her arousal cut across the air and grew stronger as they plunged into the darkened trees.

His gut twisted with guilt even as his mouth watered to taste her blueberries-and-cream scent himself. How could he lust after a girl whose father he might have to kill? How could any part of him think about holding her body against his, all soft skin and heated breaths, when his mission was to convince her to betray her father? He had done a lot of bad things in his life, but sleeping with a girl and then killing her father was *not* going to be numbered among them.

No. He was here to do exactly what he said— teach her what it meant to be a wolf. So she would understand what she truly was and what was truly at risk. He pulled her to a stop as they reached the clearing where they had first met.

"What are you going to teach me first?" she asked, breathless, standing too close and looking up into his eyes too much flirtation. She wanted to be with him, that much was obvious, although it perplexed him. She was beautiful—she could have any man she wanted—and for all he knew, she had a boyfriend already. She was unmarried and obviously unmated, but that didn't mean there wasn't someone in her life. So, why the attraction? Maybe it was simply the allure of a strange man, a shifter. Something exotic that her human side had yet to try.

He took a step back and set his face to seriousness. He could see the disappointment draw down her body.

"I saw you shift before," he said. "Your wolf is unique."

Her eyebrows lifted. "Unique how?" She seemed genuinely to have no idea, but she was open and curious about it. That was a good start.

"I've never seen a white wolf before," he explained.

"Really?" She scrunched up her face, and it

brought out that innocence again. "Your wolf was black, right? Or dark brown? It was hard to tell in the moonlight."

"Something like that. Most wolves are somewhere on the spectrum of brown to black to gray. Occasionally red. I've heard of white wolves, but they're rare."

She spread her arms wide with a wicked grin on her face. "My wolf must be *extra* magical and special." There was a laugh in her voice.

"I didn't say that." But it almost wrenched a smile out of him. It was painful, so he stopped. "Go ahead and shift. We'll run together."

"Where will we run? I mean, I'm not going to be able to talk to you once I shift, so… what's the plan?"

He couldn't help the tiny grin that snuck onto his face. "Just shift, and you'll see."

She scowled at him, but it was playful, then she stepped back, dropped her arms, and shifted into the brilliant white wolf he had seen the night before. Her clothes lay in a heap next to her. He shifted, leaving his clothes behind as well, and padded toward her. She was small and delicate-boned even as a wolf. Her paws were so tiny, he could cover two of hers with one of his. He trotted until he was nose to nose with her, and for a moment, he was captured by her brilliant blue eyes. The shadows of the trees drew into the meadow like black daggers, but her eyes sparkled in the waning sunlight.

He dropped his muzzle down to hers, and lightly touched the tip, giving her a gentle wolfish kiss. A tremor traveled the length of her body, bristling out her white fur. A spike in her arousal cut through the crisp, cooling smell of the forest.

He jerked back. What was he doing?

He shook his head to clear it. Then he linked a thought to her. *In wolf form, we don't need to speak out loud.*

She jumped back and violently shook all over, as if she could fling the thoughts right out. He sat down in the grass, holding still again and waiting for her to regain her composure.

What in the—how can you—what was that? Her thoughts were a whirl.

I can only link a thought to you across a certain distance, he thought. *Run to the far side of the meadow. See if you can hear me from there.*

She stood stiffly and stared at him, blinking once, twice. Then she took off. His wolf wanted to charge after her, perhaps tackle her and pin her, playfully of course. Maybe not so playful after that.

He stayed where he was.

Can you hear me? she thought, pausing and throwing a look back. She was only halfway across.

Keep going.

She darted off again and reached the edge of the forest in no time. His heart lurched when it appeared she might plunge into the darkened trees without him…

Grace! Don't go into the trees. He sent the command her way, but she was out of range.

She stopped anyway, then turned and looked back at him. The mere idea of her disappearing into the forest without him had him pounding hard across the meadow. At the same time, she turned to lope back toward him.

So damn sexy, I wonder if— He heard the exact moment when she came back into range.

So you think I'm sexy, huh? he replied, panting as he ran.

She screeched to a halt and dipped her head, not meeting his gaze. *Shit! This thought reading thing… how do I turn it off?*

His wolf barked a huffy kind of laugh—it felt

strange and wheezy in his chest, like cobwebs were clearing out.

She looked up, a pained expression on her face. *It's possible I'm going to die of embarrassment.*

He wheezed the barking laugh to a standstill, then trotted up to where she had stopped, stiff-legged in the middle of the meadow. *Don't worry. You'll learn to control it. I don't want to hear most of the things my brothers think, so I generally tune them out. But there are times that it's important or necessary, like on a mission. And it can be… enjoyable, like when I'm with my mate…* His own thoughts short-circuited with that idea. Those days with Avery—they were like a dream that happened and then died. She had been slender and beautiful, like Grace, only Avery was an alpha female. She knew who she was and what she wanted, and when they linked thoughts while they made love—

No! He physically shook his head and stumbled back until he nearly fell. Thinking about Avery was a dark hole that would swallow him.

Grace had recoiled from his shouted thought.

He blinked at her, flummoxed about what thought to send next.

He has a mate? Is that why… I should have known… Of course… Her thoughts were a jumble.

My mate is dead. The thought seemed to freeze both of them in a timeless moment. It stretched until he couldn't bear it any longer. He forced his body to unlock and turn away. He ran across the field toward his clothes.

This was a bad idea. He couldn't do this. The unsteady feeling had him nearly tripping on his way, desperate in his need to get back to his clothes, shift human, take her home, walk away, and… come back later tonight and simply end it. Kill the Senator. Go to jail. Stop all of it.

Stop coming apart at the seams.

He heard her paws in the grass, trying to keep up with him. He had worked up to a full sprint without realizing it. He didn't slow down. When he reached his clothes, he shifted. He clenched his fists to work out the shakes, then struggled at getting his clothes on, keeping his head down as he did.

Grace shifted human next to him, but he didn't look. Couldn't look at her anymore. Needed to get away. Get her home then…

She touched his arm.

He jerked back, one leg in his pants, one out, half stumbling.

She pulled back and gathered her hair around

her nakedness, caving her body in to cover the parts that spoke to his wolf.

Her voice was a pained whisper. "I'm sorry, Jared. I didn't know."

It was the soft concern on her face that undid him. The gentleness, the expression full of empathy, echoing feelings he couldn't hold in his chest without being destroyed by them... she gathered them up and held them in her own, just by being near him. By spending a moment in his thoughts.

He ducked his head. "Not your fault. It's mine." It was *all* his fault, even now. He finished pulling on his pants, roughly tugging them in place. He didn't look at her. He wanted her to stay away.

She came closer.

He could see her bare feet in the grass.

Then she touched him again, a whisper of softness against his arm. The melting feeling was back, and he couldn't move, as if liquid cement had trickled through his body and glued him in place. Slowly, very slowly, he raised his gaze to her brilliant blue eyes.

"Why did you really come back?" she asked, softly. Gentle as the breeze kissing the grass and bending the stalks. She searched his face with those eyes, then gave him a bashful smile. "I had this silly hope that maybe you came back for *me*. That maybe I'd be getting my first kiss from a shifter—"

"You don't want me as your first for anything." The cold was seeping back into his bones. Freezing him tight. Sealing up the seams. "I'm a bad man, Grace. I've killed people."

She frowned but didn't pull away. "You're military, aren't you?"

He squinted to see her better, backdropped by the rising moon. Did she know who he was? "Ex-Marine. Sharp-shooter."

She nodded. "Fighting for your country doesn't make you bad."

"Sometimes it does." The words were out of his mouth before he could stop them.

She frowned again, but this time like he was a puzzle. "You came back because you wanted something. What is it?"

He pulled away from her. "You know about your father's shifter legislation, don't you?"

She nodded.

"Do you understand what it means? What it will do to shifters everywhere?"

She scowled and caved in more on herself, wrapping her arms in front of her chest. "I know it's bad. I've fought him on it. There's nothing I can do."

He gritted his teeth and scooped his shirt off the ground. "Fight harder. People's lives are at risk."

Her arms dropped to her sides, fists clenched. "Don't you think I've tried? *I'm* a shifter, too. You know, in case you haven't noticed. It's going to kill everything I've worked for."

He glared at her. "Then stop him."

"I can't!" Her lips pouted, and she suddenly looked young to him. Too young to really under-stand how much would be lost in this.

He stepped back further. "Then we're done here. Get your clothes."

She growled and spun around to stomp after her clothes buried in the grass. He watched as she tugged on her silky blouse and narrow skirt. They had ditched her fancy, politician's daughter shoes before they snuck out of the house. When she was done dressing, she stomped off toward the trees, on her way back to the estate.

He hesitated, but only for a moment, then he jogged after her. The icy chill inside him was stitching him back together again. He should escort her back to the house, return to his perch, and end this thing tonight. But as she picked her way through the brambles, cursing at the branches as they tugged at her clothes, he knew—he wasn't killing her father. Not tonight. Not until he had done everything he could to win her over.

And he'd done a really shitty job of that so far.

She stopped at the edge of the forest, still out of sight of anyone happening to glance their way from the estate. Only then did he see the tracks of tears glistening on her cheeks. It gave him that loose feeling again, like the world was tipping.

She turned to him, eyes glassy and angry. "We have a week."

"A week. What happens in a week?"

"In a week, my father announces his run for re-election on a platform of requiring shifters to register on the grounds of public safety. He's going to criminalize every last one of you."

"Every last one of *us.*" He held her gaze.

"Every last one of *you,*" she said, harshly. "*Me,* he will disown and kick out on the streets."

"You're his daughter," he said softly. "If you tell him—"

"He hates you! Loathes you with every fiber of his being. Trust me, when he finds out, it will be *far* easier for him to get rid of a daughter than to abandon his Senate seat."

A growl rumbled in his chest. "How could any man do that to his daughter?"

But her shoulders just dropped, and she gave a forlorn look at the house.

It tore at him. "Tell him," Jared said softly. "You might be surprised."

She just shook her head.

Then something occurred to him. He wasn't sure why he didn't see it before. "He must have loved a shifter once," he said, very gently.

She frowned at him. "What are you talking about?"

"He has *you.*" Jared nodded. This had to be the answer.

"I told you, it won't matter. He's too stubborn."

"But he's not a shifter himself, right?" he prompted.

She leaned back and gave him a look like he was crazy. "Well, that would be pretty odd, don't you think?"

"Stranger things have happened." He waited for her to figure it out, but she was shaking her head, dazed. "If you are a shifter, and your father is not, then…"

Her eyes widened. "What are you saying?"

He huffed a laugh. "Do I really have to spell it out for you?"

But her eyes just got wider. "My mother was *not* a shifter."

"Are you sure?"

"*Yes,* I'm sure." Her eyes were tearing up again.

"Well, *one* of your parents is."

Her mouth fell open, and all the color drained from her face as she stared at the house. "Please tell me…" She looked back at him, stricken. "Please tell me there's some kind of recessive gene. Some way I could get some of it from both of them, but not have either one of them actually, you know, be a wolf."

He frowned, finally figuring out why this was freaking her out—*she might not be the Senator's daughter after all.* "Grace, it's not a recessive trait. I… I wish I could tell you differently. You can be half wolf and still be able to shift, but anything less than that… at least one of your parents is a full shifter. "

She stared at the house again. "One week." Then she turned back to him. "We have one week to stop this."

He nodded and followed her determined stride back to the house.

Chapter Six

GRACE WAS WEARING HER TYPICAL, TRIM BUSINESS attire. Her hair was neatly bound up, her silk blouse was tucked into her slim skirt, and her three-inch heels made her tall enough to look Jared, her new bodyguard, in the eyes. Only she hadn't been able to look him in the face since he picked her up this morning from the estate.

Everything in her life was unraveling.

Jared trailed behind her as she strode, as confidently as she could, into the high-rise that held her father's campaign office. Jared wore the same dark suit as last night, his jacket and white dress shirt neatly tailored to fit his large, muscular body. He'd kept absolutely silent on the long drive into downtown. He clearly had issues of his own, and she didn't know where any of this was going, but she still was having a full-body-alert reaction to his nearness. It surged up her wolf, and twice already this morning, Grace was afraid she would accidentally shift. Her wolf gave a constant whimper of need that was utterly distracting. And whenever Grace accidentally touched him—when he gave her a hand to climb out of her father's black sedan, when she accidentally brushed him as he held the door, or just now, as they both reached for the elevator button at the same time—it was like electricity zapping through her body.

Jared dropped his gaze and pulled back from the elevator buttons. He was so tightly wound. Grace didn't know what roiled under that cool, calm exterior, but she'd seen a glimpse of it the night before, when he said his mate was dead. There was so much pain and grief, and he'd locked it down so quickly—the idea of being with him seemed like being around a ticking bomb. Only she wasn't afraid. More like she wanted to defuse it, take it apart, see what was inside. In spite of the mess she was in, this mysterious shifter was strangely exciting… albeit in a "you might die from the explosion" kind of way.

Jared held the campaign office door open for

her. She strode in ahead of him, heading straight for her little-used office and ducking her head to avoid Kylie's goggle-eyed looks and Nolan's narrow-eyed suspicion. She held the door of her office for Jared, then closed it behind him. That would hold Kylie and Nolan off for at least a minute.

She stayed by the door, arms crossed. "Are you going to talk to me?"

He strolled over to her desk, scanning the office with a calculated look. "I was waiting until we had a moment alone."

"We've been alone for the forty-five minute drive into the city." She wasn't sure why she was poking him, or that she even wanted to talk, but his silence was driving her nuts.

"I was waiting until we were alone *and* I wasn't operating heavy machinery I might crash."

That drew a small smile out of her. "Why don't you start by telling me your real name? I know it's not Jared Bachman, or whatever you told my father."

"Does it matter?" His dark-eyed stare zoomed in hard on her. "You already know more about me than you need to."

So that was how it was going to be. "I don't know anywhere near what I need to." She stalked away from the door and stood close to him, staring defiantly up into his dark eyes, her hands clenched at her side. "You want me to give up everything that I have—my job, my home, my father's love…" She stalled out, choking up. "You *know* he's going to toss me out as soon as he figures out I'm not really his child."

Jared's hard stare melted a little, but she pressed on. She was just getting started.

"All that," she said, getting up her steam, "and you won't even tell me your name? Who are you really? Who are you working for? And don't they have someone better at this job they could send to convince me to give up everything for your cause?"

The hardness returned to his eyes. "Yes, there are other people who could do this. People who would blackmail you. Use your secret to force you to do what's right. I was hoping—no, I made the apparent error in thinking—that you might do the right thing on your own, once you understood the stakes."

Anger was welling up inside her. *"The right thing?"* Her voice was rising. "I'm *trying* to do the right thing! I'm trying to find a way out of this. Can't you see I want to stop my father and this terrible idea of his?"

He gave her a look of disgust. "You're trying to remain, if at all possible, the pampered daughter of a Senator, even though you're a shifter. You don't care what happens to everyone else."

She actually raised her clenched fists, as if she could pummel this large, muscular, dangerously sexy man who was demanding impossible things of her. "I'm doing the best that I can!"

His voice was cool, with a slightly raised eyebrow for her threatening fists. "I'm sure that will be a consolation to all the shifters whose lives are ruined by your father's legislation."

Her fists dropped, and her shoulders slumped. He was right. Her life didn't really matter—well it mattered a lot to *her*, but she had spent her whole life trying to help others, and when it really came down to it, all she could think about was the fact that her mother had cheated on her father. With a shifter. And created her, this half-shifter illegitimate child.

Her life was unraveling.

His voice was soft again. "Why are we here, Grace?"

She didn't look at him, just shook her head, staring at the floor. "It's better if I go about my normal activities until we figure this out." Her voice felt hollow, and her skin was too tight. There was no way out of this box, and even if there were, she wouldn't be able to find it—her head was still spinning too much. And her heart felt like it was breaking.

Jared lifted a hand to her shoulder. His hand was big and heavy, and it felt like he could crush her with a single squeeze, but his touch was gentle and warm. Completely unlike the hard-eyed anger from before.

"I'm sorry about your parents," he said. "I'd assumed that you'd figured it out already. I should've known better—you've been isolated. On your own. It doesn't have to be that way, not for our kind. Wolves are built to be part of a pack, Grace. I know you don't have one, but that's why I'm here. To help you see what you need to do."

She looked up into his eyes—they had turned warm. The electric feel of him touching her was even stronger now with his soft words. She leaned into him a little.

"I can't believe my mom had an affair. It's just... I don't even know who I am anymore."

"I know how that feels," he said in a whisper. His hand on her shoulder squeezed a little —he was so strong, that small movement pulled her closer, until her body was nearly touching his. His eyes went a little round, like he hadn't meant to do that. Every part of her was heating with his nearness. Her chest was tight with need, and she thought maybe he wanted to kiss her. She sure as hell wanted to kiss him. Wanted to have some relief from this constant sexual tension, something to distract her, blur her mind, and make her forget about everything. But her mind was too mixed up to tell if it was all in her head, or if he was feeling it, too.

She didn't get a chance to find out because, at that exact moment, Kylie burst through the door.

"Oh!" Kylie exclaimed, screeching to a halt by the door. "Er… good morning… Grace and the extremely large man who is accompanying her."

Jared dropped his hand from her shoulder and backed away. Grace turned slowly and gave her best friend a look she hoped would vaporize her on the spot.

Kylie beamed an even larger smile. "I'm having trouble with the coffee maker, Grace! Can you come work your magic on it?"

Grace blew out her frustration in a low breath. Kylie's curiosity was burning, and Grace knew she would have to explain anyway, so she might as well get it over with.

She glanced back to Jared. "Duty calls."

He squinted at her in a way that said he wasn't amused, but he let her go with a nod.

Grace led the way from her office to the tiny closet that served as a coffee room. Kylie was hot on her heels. Nolan caught sight of them and hustled over. There was hardly room for the three of them to stand in the cramped closet, but Kylie jammed them all inside and closed the door.

"Oh my God, Grace! Is that *him?*" Kylie gushed.

Nolan scowled. "Him who? There's a *him?* I haven't heard of a him before."

"The guy Grace is hot for!" Kylie shushed him, then turned to Grace. "That's him, isn't it?"

Nolan swung to her. "You're hot for that guy?" The jealousy was rolling off him in waves, and Grace really didn't need to deal with *that* on top of everything else.

"Jesus, Nolan," she said. "I can't help it if the man's hot."

"So you *do* think he's hot?" His pinched look got even more so.

"She has a pulse, doesn't she?" Kylie whacked his chest with the back of her hand. "Back off,

Nolan. The girl has a Grade-A hottie in her grasp. Don't mess it up."

"When did all this happen?" Nolan was gritting his teeth. "Since when do you have a boyfriend?"

"He's not my boyfriend," Grace said, wearily. She couldn't even see a word as tame as *boyfriend* applying to Jared. "His name is Jared, and he's my new bodyguard."

Kylie squeaked and clapped her hands together. "Holy shit, that's even better! Jesus, Grace, why do you get all the lucky breaks?"

Grace glared at her. "It's not lucky to have a need for a personal bodyguard."

Nolan frowned. "Hang on, why do you need a bodyguard all of a sudden?"

Some of the glee finally dropped off Kylie's face. "Wait a minute, is something wrong?"

Grace took a deep breath, but she figured that lie was the simplest of all. "There's some shifter gangs out there who aren't happy with my father. Apparently, there been some threats against me. My father wanted me to have a personal bodyguard, just in case."

Kylie's face took on a look of horror. "Oh my God, Grace."

Nolan's face had gone stormy. "What kind of threats?"

"I'm sure it's nothing."

"I'm sure it's *not* nothing." Nolan's storm darkened. "The Senator wouldn't do this if it weren't necessary."

Grace shook her head. Her father, the Senator, was looking out for himself, primarily. That would be even more true, if he knew what she was.

"I don't like this." Nolan's voice had dropped an octave.

"Well, I don't like it, either," Grace said. "It's probably nothing, but I'm going to have a bodyguard for a while, so you guys will have to get used to it. Just for the campaign. Just a precaution."

"I think I need to have a talk with your new bodyguard." Nolan wrestled the door open and squeezed past them to get out.

"Oh Christ," Grace said under her breath.

Kylie scowled after him. "He better not mess with this. You need to get laid, Grace, and Hot Bodyguard Man seems like just the ticket. Don't worry, I won't let Nolan screw this up for you." She charged out after him.

Grace sighed and followed them both, scurrying in her high heels to try to stop Nolan before he reached Jared. But by the time she arrived at her office, Nolan was already laying into Jared, who was looming over him with his arms crossed. Jared's expression, looking down at Nolan, was the kind you gave a steaming pile of crap on the sidewalk that you'd like to avoid stepping in.

Nolan was getting in his face. "What kind of threat are we talking here? Do you have the details? Or are you just the muscle?"

"Nolan!" Grace said, stumbling into the room. "For God's sake—"

"We have a right to know," Nolan said, throwing a glance at her. "If there's a threat against you, and you bring it into the office, we have to know what we're dealing with." He mimicked Jared by folding his arms.

"Nolan, don't be a pain in the ass." But Kylie's admonishment didn't even make him flinch.

"Shifters are dangerous," Nolan said, his voice hard. "If it's a gang, it's even worse. If it's some deranged individual, with a burr in his fur, they could be flat psychotic. A predator. They're animals, and God only knows what they'll do. So I want to hear everything you know about this threat against Grace." Nolan's words were hard and demanding—

Grace was impressed that Jared kept his expression unchanging and inscrutable.

"You're the speechwriter, right?" Jared's voice was ice cold.

"What does that have to do with anything—"

"No one cares about you."

Grace had to stifle her laugh. She really shouldn't be laughing—Nolan was just trying to protect her. Well, throw his testosterone around a bit, like he was marking territory or something, but also protect her. She knew him—he was genuinely worried. And he had cause to be, only not for the reasons he thought.

Meanwhile, Nolan's face was slowly turning red. "Maybe they're trying to intimidate us. Maybe this threat from the shifters is all about derailing the Senator's plans." He swung a pointed look to Grace. "We're not going to let them intimidate us, are we, Grace?"

Jared flicked a look at her, boring into her with his dark eyes.

"That's why I'm here," Grace said to both of them. "We continue on, just like normal. We don't let anyone intimidate us."

She pursed her lips because she didn't really want to have this conversation at all.

ALISA WOODS

Nolan and Kylie were both giving her nods of approval. Nolan unlocked his arms and strode toward the door. He brushed past her, giving her a still-angry look, but then he paused at the threshold. "We have that rally at two o'clock. I'm going. Kylie will go. But Grace… I think you should stay here."

She shook her head. "No, I'll be there."

He frowned and raked a harsh look over Jared. "Make sure you bring the muscle." Then he stalked out of the room.

Kylie rolled her eyes. "Ignore him," she said to Grace. Then she grinned and crossed the room to offer her hand to Jared. He jumped a little, then slowly extended his to shake.

"My name's Kylie. You just let me know if you need anything. Anything at all." She gave him one of her patented *please bed me* smiles, then turned and sauntered from the room.

Grace closed the door behind her.

"Your boyfriend?" Jared asked coolly.

"Ex-boyfriend. He's a nice guy."

"He's not a nice guy, Grace. He's a bigot. And if he knew what you were, he'd fear and hate you just like all the rest. That's what we're up against."

Grace leaned back against the door. "I know." She pressed the heels of her hands to her forehead

94

and closed her eyes. "I need coffee. And time to sort this out." Then she opened her eyes. "Are you really going to hang out in the office here with me all day?"

He gave her a very small smile—it wouldn't have been a big deal on anyone else, except that she'd never seen a real smile on his face. It looked like it hurt him. "I'm your bodyguard."

She snorted a laugh. "All right, Mr. Jared, the bodyguard with no last name. Make yourself useful and get me some coffee, will you?"

He gave her a small scowl, but it wasn't too harsh. "You're trying to get rid of me."

She sighed. "Only for a minute. You can bring your badass self back here if you've got coffee."

That small smile made an appearance again, then he strode toward the door. She stepped aside to let him pass, but when she closed the door again, she banged her head softly against it.

One week. Six days now, actually.

She had to pull herself together enough to fix this mess.

Chapter Seven

JARED SHOULD HAVE KNOWN—THE RALLY AT 2 o'clock was an anti-shifter one.

He stood to Grace's right, while the ex-boyfriend speechwriter stood to her left, and the coordinator girl—he thought her name was Kylie—flitted around the stage and fussed with the Senator's microphone.

Every muscle in Jared's body clenched.

The restless crowd that had gathered in the rented hall quietly murmured amongst themselves, waiting to hear the main speaker—two others had already spouted more hate speech than Jared wanted to hear in a lifetime. They were ordinary folk, just as he always suspected—that neighbor down the street, the guy you buy your groceries from, the mid-level manager coming down from her office for a little bigotry with her lunch. Their hatred was a pheromone that floated in the air—the scent of their anger twisted his stomach. Evil was a common enough thing in the world, but he thought he'd left most of it overseas. To see so much of it on display in Seattle chilled him deep in his bones.

He kept quiet, not blowing his cover in front of the speechwriter, but that asshole sure was flapping in his mouth.

"Would you look at the size of this crowd?" Nolan held up both hands as if embracing the lot of them.

Grace bent her head to listen, and with her hair pulled back, Jared could see the tight press of her lips. He would give anything to know what she was thinking, but that would have to wait until later. Assuming this poison didn't seep into her system and scare her off.

Nolan kept talking. "The poll numbers are off the charts. People don't want to say it out loud, but they're starting to. Look at this…" He gestured to the crowd again. "This is on a Tuesday afternoon. Think about what it'll look like when we have an evening rally, or a weekend one."

Grace just shook her head and didn't answer.

The Senator tapped the microphone, and the crowd quieted down. He started in on his speech, which Jared had absolutely no interest in. He watched Grace instead. Her eyes were glued to her father's tall, commanding form. He was almost big enough to be a shifter, and a nagging doubt tugged at Jared's mind. Was it possible? He seriously doubted it. There were plenty of alpha males in the human population who weren't alpha because of their wolf nature. Which Jared actually counted against them. Wolves were more pure in spirit than humans—at least, Jared's wolf nature was the good side of him, as far as he could tell. It was his human hands who had done all the killing, and humans who had given him the orders to do it. Humans made war; not wolves. Packs only fought when a member was threatened. It wasn't as if there weren't dark wolves—there were—but usually it was the human side corrupting the wolf, not the other way around.

No, the Senator wasn't good enough to be a shifter.

"They're a hidden menace among us," he was intoning, to murmurs of agreement in the crowd. "They're overrepresented in our criminal elements, they hide in the shadows, and by their very nature, they're dangerous. They don't reason or think the way humans do—they make blood vows within their packs and revel in their aggressive, animal nature. It's not entirely their fault, I understand that. They can't help being born what they are. But that doesn't erase the fact that they're a danger to the law-abiding citizens of our country."

The crowd cheered, and the Senator paused, obviously relishing their adulation. His words made Jared wish he had pulled the trigger. But the look on Grace's face—a scowl that grew darker with each line of the speech—reminded him why he didn't. If only he could convince her that she could stop all this. He'd seen enough of her already to know she was strong, and she had a purity of heart about her —her wolf was hard to contain, and that brought out her righteous side. The question was whether she would be strong enough to stand up to the alpha male in her life—her father. Jared could see the dynamic: the Senator dominated everyone around him, including his daughter.

The man was still droning on with his speech. "The time is coming, my friends, very soon. We need to do something about this, take action that will ensure the safety of the good people of Seattle and Washington. Your numbers here today are heartening to me. You've taken time from your day, your lives, your work in making this country strong, to show your support for keeping it that way. I want you to know that I am on your side. And in the days to come, I hope you'll be on mine."

The Senator was wrapping up—thank God—but the crowd seemed far from ready to be done.

Nolan was clapping along with everyone else. He leaned over to Grace. "Do you see this?"

She nodded. "Do they really believe all this stuff?"

Jared whipped his attention to her.

"Hell yeah, they do," Nolan said. "I took half this speech straight from the online sites where they rant about this stuff all the time. It's what the people believe, Grace, and remember… we represent the people."

"What happened to doing what's right?" She was scowling at the crowd, not even looking at Nolan.

"What's right for who?" He pulled back and gave her a frown. "I'm all for protecting the people —if they're innocent. Shifters aren't innocent bystanders in this, Grace. They're involved in the drug trade, weapons dealing, who knows what else. They're legitimately dangerous. You wouldn't let convicted criminals run around in the streets, would you?"

"I'm not saying that, and you know it, Nolan." She turned her scowl on him.

Nolan's determination faltered. He leaned toward her. "It's what your father wants, Grace. And I want to keep my job."

She gave him a pinched look, but Nolan dropped his gaze and moved across the stage toward the Senator. He was already walking down the three steps into the crowd to shake hands.

Grace stayed where she was.

"He's kind of an asshole," Jared said.

"He's not. He's a good man."

"Doesn't look that way from my angle." Jared studied how Nolan moved through the crowd, following in the wake of the Senator, pressing flesh with people and chatting them up. "He looks pretty comfortable in the hate crowd."

The sound of a hundred conversations was making it so that he had to speak up, but it also meant his voice wouldn't carry. A few people trickled in and out of the two sets of doors—one in back and one off to the side—but for the most part, people were grabbing cups of coffee from the refreshment tables and hanging around for more hater chit-chat.

Jared couldn't wait to leave, but he wasn't budging from Grace's side.

She turned to peer up at him with her bright blue eyes. "Nolan's just doing his job."

"I've used that excuse, too."

She frowned. "What happened to you? When you were in the military, something happened."

"This isn't about me," he said coolly. He already told her what he was—she didn't need to know he had one of the highest kill counts in Afghanistan. "This is about you, and whether you're going to do what's right, or if you're just going to do your job, like your ex-boyfriend."

Grace's eyes unfocused as she gazed out into the crowd, watching Nolan again.

Jared sensed an opportunity, a moment—she was faltering. He could feel it. "You're not one of these people, Grace. They would string you up if they could. They're already doing medical experiments on people like you and me."

Her pretty face whipped back to his. *"What?"*

He dropped his voice to just below the murmur of the crowd, so she had to lean in to hear him. "Civilian shifters. Military shifters. There are already people in the government who feel free to kidnap them and perform experiments. They're *already* treating us like we're subhuman—your father is just trying to make it legal."

Her face twisted up, horrified. "How is that even possible?"

"I saw it with my own eyes. I was one of the ones taken, but I didn't suffer anywhere near as much as some. There are a few who've died; several more on their way. Tortured, kept in cages."

Her expression just got more and more disbelieving—no, she believed him. That was why she was so horrified. "Why don't you tell someone? Why not go public with this?"

"We might. Probably will. But there are lots of people in high positions of power protecting this, orchestrating it. We have reason to believe your father is involved."

"*No.*" She actually took a step back this time, almost like she was losing her balance.

Jared instinctively reached for her, caught her by the elbow, and kept her upright.

She was shaking her head. "No. Stop it. Stop saying these things." She jerked her elbow out of his grasp.

"I'm only saying what's true, Grace." He hated

doing this to her. It was tearing him up inside to see that look on her face. His wolf surged up with the need to protect her, even if it was from the truth about her father. And herself.

She shook her head more violently, then turned away from him. Her heels clacked across the wood floor of the raised stage.

Shit. He was driving her away—too much, too soon. And just like in the meadow, the image of her retreating back—her fleeing *away* from him— surged up the need to go after her. Knowing he was causing her this pain, while the same time knowing that it had to be done… it was opening the fissures inside him again.

She pounded down the stairs. He grimaced, hesitated, then went after her, cursing himself for handling the whole thing so badly.

She pushed her way through the crowd. The haters made space for the pretty Senator's daughter, and she left mystified looks in her wake. Jared trudged after her, calculating where he could corner her and explain. Or maybe backpedal. Soften it somehow. This had to be hard for her, and he *had* to find a way to make it work. To bring her over to his side. Because the alternative was worse than anything she was feeling right now.

When she reached the side door, a man in a hoodie who was lounging against the wall suddenly grabbed her and wrapped his arm around her neck to hold her firm against his chest.

Shock rippled through Jared, and he nearly shifted… but he managed to keep it under control and sprinted toward the man instead. A scream went up near the main door, and movement burst through the hall—a whole group of these hooded men sprung to life and fanned out into the crowd. They were large and hulking—too oversized to be casual hatemongers. Were these *shifters?* What the hell were they doing? Jared growled, cursing whatever was about to go down, but his focus stayed on Grace and the man holding her. She was terrified, clawing her hands at the man's arm around her throat. Jared had to push his way through the now-panicked crowd.

The hooded man wasn't choking her, just holding her and forcing her to watch whatever was going down, but it made Jared want to rip off his face. He finally pushed past the last of the attendees and lunged up to them, plowing his fist to the guy's nose. The shock of it, and the crunch of the man's nose breaking under his knuckles, made Grace scream and the man's grip on her slacken. He slumped to the ground. Jared gathered Grace into his arms, protectively, and her small body melted against his chest. He turned her away from the crowd and trapped her body against the wall, covering her with his bulk before finally twisting around to see what else was happening.

His heart thudded, as he quickly took in the scene—the hooded men were shouting, intimidating the crowd, and shoving people to the floor, but the only blood he saw was on the man's face at his feet. The mayhem was distracting everyone from the one guy who was moving toward the front. He had something in his hands, and for a moment Jared thought it was a bomb—but then the man shook it and started spraying the wall behind the podium. It was a gang symbol—a shifter gang Jared recognized—and the words, *we're watching you.*

What the hell?

The man let out a whistle, and the rest scattered, making for the exits. One stopped to hoist up the bloodied man at Jared's feet—he was dazed but not completely knocked out. Jared stared long and hard at their faces as they hurried out the doors and into the Seattle afternoon sun.

He had no idea who they were, but he was

damn sure they weren't shifters. And he wasn't at all surprised when the Senator took the podium again.

"Everyone please remain calm and see if anyone around you is hurt. The shifter gang appears to have left, although their message is clear. But we will not be intimidated by lawlessness and violence! I promise you, we will find who is responsible for this."

Jared snarled. This was an obvious setup to anyone with eyes to see, but there was no one in the room who would dispute it. The gang whose symbol was dripping paint would be blamed—even though that made no sense at all for a gang to come here and tag up the place. But the Senator would use it as leverage to whip his troops into a frenzy. And get voters to the polls.

Grace was shaking in his arms. He instinctively pulled her closer and pressed her head against his chest. Her gulping breaths slowly calmed.

"You're okay, Grace. I've got you." She nodded against his chest. That feeling of her moving against him, of her accepting his desire to protect her, surged his wolf twice as strong as before. He wanted nothing more than to haul her away from this place and never return. She needed to be *gone* from all of this, and he needed to have her, like this, in his arms.

And more.

That urge—that *need* for her—stunned him so badly, he actually loosened his grip and took a step back.

She looked at him with wide eyes.

He still held her shoulders. "Are you all right?" he asked, wanting to draw her back, but not daring to do it. He would end up kissing her. And then everything would come apart inside him.

She nodded quickly, and the color seemed to be returning to her face. She smoothed out her blouse and tucked it back into her skirt. She gave him a nod, then turned toward the podium where her father was still reassuring the crowd.

Jared needed to get her alone. Soon. He told himself it was just to talk, to convince her to leave. With him. But he knew it was more than that.

This desire for her felt dangerous, like he was on the edge of a precipice about to fall.

And he *wanted* to fall… all the way down.

Which surprised him most of all.

Chapter Eight

GRACE'S HANDS HAD STOPPED THEIR SHAKING, BUT she was still quivering inside.

Jared drove her father's black sedan through the winding mountain roads toward her father's estate. He sat in front, eyes on the road, as she rode in back, watching the beloved forest of her youth slip by—a steady, vision-blurring stream of green pine needles, woody trunks, and leafy undergrowth. Her body buzzed along with the whizzing scenery, numbed by the events at the rally.

So much had gone down in such a short period of time, it was like her body was in shock. Her mind, on the other hand, was going a million miles an hour. Her father's legislation—the one she had been fighting for months—was tapping into the fears of a rabid set of people. Their hate-filled faces; their palpable anger; these were her father's foot soldiers. *His voters.* These were the people who would cheer on his attempt to criminalize a whole swath of people.

People like her.

At the beginning of the rally, as the hall had filled to capacity, a sickening dread had trickled through her like ice water in her veins—it was a raw fear that somehow she would be discovered. That this horde of angry people would realize what she was. It was a *personal* fear, one for her own safety, even her life. One she hadn't felt before... *ever.* She watched Jared's stone-cold face turn into something even more hard and bitter—he wasn't afraid, but she could see the flickers of anger below that inscrutable, chiseled expression. He'd known exactly who these people were and what they were capable of... and yet he stood by her side, unafraid to face them, so he could appeal to her and try to convince her that she should fight them.

Her fear had made her ashamed. Eventually, the disgust rose up to push the fear and shame aside, especially with Nolan's obvious pandering. He would use these people and their anger just like her father would—to keep his job and increase his power. All along, Grace thought they were all driven by the same thing—a sense of justice. A desire to make the world a better place for the people living in it. That kind of power was invigorating, to be sure, but only because it was the power to do *good* in the world. But what seethed in that hall was the opposite—that hatred was the raw fuel for political power, and it would drive her father's ascendancy in the world, along with all his minions, including Nolan.

Grace wanted to believe she would have still seen the *wrongness* of it, even if she wasn't a shifter herself… but she wasn't entirely sure. Nolan seemed to know it was wrong, but that didn't stop him from following her father, wading into the crowd to glad-hand and win more votes. It was Nolan's easy acceptance of all of it that had shocked her the most. Then Jared's blazing words about some kind of government experiments on shifters, then the attack… and suddenly her shock had gone into overdrive, leaving her in this buzzed state as Jared whisked her from the rally, stuffing her in the sedan and hurrying them away. She hadn't even asked where they were going, but she quickly realized he was taking her home… only it didn't feel like *home* any longer.

ALISA WOODS

It felt like a place she no longer fit.

Jared pulled the car up to the front door of the estate. She fumbled with the car door handle, but she couldn't seem to get it to work. Her hands were still shaking after all. Jared hurried around to open her door. His hand clasped hers, enveloping it in his hot-skinned touch… even the look in his eyes had warmed from before, at the rally. He grasped hold of her arm to keep her steady, and she almost protested, but his calm command, guiding her toward the house and making sure she was steady on her feet, was settling the shaking in her hands, so she didn't. Jared exchanged a rapid-yet-silent communication with Richard, the guard on duty— he took the car while Jared escorted her inside.

It made her feel cared for in a way that cleared her mind.

She and Jared needed to talk.

His large form hovered, strong but gentle, next to hers as he ushered her through the house.

"Do you need something to drink or eat?" he asked quietly as they passed the kitchen.

"No." Her voice still had a tremble in it. She took a deep breath and blew it out slowly. They kept going past the kitchen, and it was clear he was steering her toward her bedroom—which flushed her face with heat as she thought of the things she'd fantasized about doing there with him. None of which was appropriate at the moment.

Jared closed the bedroom door behind him, then without a word, he shucked off his jacket and drew her into his arms. He held her tightly—so tight that all the tension stringing her body released at once, and she just sagged into him.

"It's okay," he said softly, his hands in her hair, gently stroking the back of her head and holding her in the secure cage of his arms. "It's over. You're all right now."

"Jared." She buried her face in his chest and bunched up his neatly-pressed dress shirt in her fist.

His hand on her stilled, and she could feel the muscles in his arms flex around her, tensing up.

She lifted her head to peer up at him. "What am I going to do?"

He was speechless, looking down at her with dark eyes that were no longer hard. His lips parted, but no words came out. For a moment, she thought he might kiss her, but then he loosened his hold and stepped back.

He still kept his hands on her shoulders. "Those men in hoods weren't shifters, Grace."

"I know." She let out a breath, glad he was still

holding onto her. Somehow it felt like he was the only thing keeping her up. "It was obvious my father hired them. To shift blame. To stir up the crowd. Probably to make the news as well." Her shoulders sagged with the weight of that truth— that was what had knocked the final, buzzing shock into her. She hadn't been afraid of the attackers. She'd been afraid to look the truth in the face—the whole thing had been an obvious manipulation for her father's political gain. It was a stinging indictment, more than almost anything else she'd seen or heard so far.

Jared squeezed her shoulders. He didn't say anything, but there was relief on his face.

"What am I going to do?" she repeated. "It's like there's suddenly a war, and I'm not sure what side I should be on." She pleaded him with her eyes —she needed him to tell her, again, why it was necessary for her to come out. Why she had to abandon everything in her life—everything her life was supposed to be—and fight this *thing* her father was doing.

"You know what side you belong on, Grace." But his voice was gentle, kind.

She shook her head, needing more. "How do I know you're telling the truth about those experiments? About my father being involved? For all I know, you're just... just making things up! Trying to convince me to betray the Senator—to ruin him by coming out as a shifter." Because that's what it would be—a PR disaster, only this time, it would be an intentional one. A self-inflicted wound that would take down her father and his plans as well.

Jared's calm expression warped into concern. "I wouldn't lie to you, Grace."

"I don't know that!" She wrenched out of his grasp because tears were glassing her eyes, and she was ashamed of them. She turned away and strode across the thick, cream-colored carpeting to the wall of windows on the far side of the room. Her bedroom was a host of barely-concealed lies—the contradictions that lay just under the skin of her life. The gymnastics trophies from when she was a girl stood proudly on her shelves—she'd always been unnaturally strong, in spite of her slender frame. *Because she was actually a wolf.* Her bed's deep purple spread was neatly tucked in, mocking her with the fact that she was twenty-five years old and never had a man in it. *Because she was a shifter.* The framed pictures of her and her father meeting important politicians, from the time she was a little girl, all the way up to meeting the Secretary of

State last month. She was the politician's daughter. His protégé. She was the goddamn campaign manager for the state's most anti-shifter politician. *And she was a shifter.*

It was all lies. And it was all going to crumble down around her and bury her along with him.

She felt Jared's presence behind her, all warmth and strength. She envied him in that moment—knowing who he was with such conviction. Having strength enough for her to borrow. It wasn't that she thought he was lying to her—far from it. She just didn't know if she had the strength to face the truth.

"Grace…" There was a ripple of pain in his voice, and it tore through her. "I don't know how to convince you that I'm telling the truth." She could hear the plea in it, and *that*—that vulnerability—was what forced her to lift her chin and turn to face him.

Because this brave, strong man was one of the shifters who would be hurt if she didn't do what was right.

"I believe you," she whispered, her lips barely moving as she stared up into his dark eyes. "But I'm afraid." She blinked back the tears. "I'm ashamed to say that, but it's true."

His hands were on her cheeks in an instant,

cupping them and holding her face tenderly. "Don't be afraid. No matter what, I'll protect you." There was *need* in his voice again, and with his hands on her cheeks, and his suddenly labored breath in her face, her pulse raced ahead. Her wolf whimpered, crying out for him to move closer, kiss her, take her like she had been imagining from that very first moment in the field.

Time suspended as he held her, stretching into long seconds. A war was taking place on Jared's face. Just as she thought he might lean in to kiss her, as she parted her lips to accept whatever he had to give, his eyes widened, and he took a step back. She instantly missed the feel of his strong hands; her wolf howled in frustration. But Jared wasn't here to kiss her—he was here to win her over to his side, politically. The *right* side, as he saw it. And as she was slowly having to admit was the only side that justice could be found on.

"You know," she said quietly, dipping her head and looking up at him through her lashes. Embarrassment heated her face. "The fantasies I've had about having you in my bedroom generally involved you ravishing me on my bed, not talking me into revolution."

His eyes went wide, he blinked, then a slow

smile quirked one side of his mouth. "Fantasies? As in *plural.*"

She huffed out a small laugh. "Just two or three. I'm not counting the one where you tie me up, because really… that's kind of unnecessary."

That look of *need* returned to his face. It forced the smile off hers… and sent a flush of heat between her legs. *Oh, God.* Her wolf was being drawn in by that look like it was a high-powered magnet.

Jared stepped closer again. "You're in danger of making me feel things, Grace. Things I haven't felt in a long time." He visibly swallowed. "I don't know what to do with that… with *you*… it's not why I'm here." He frowned. "Only it is. From the first moment I saw you shift, when I realized what you were and the situation you were in, it's like you reached inside me and… well, I haven't been able to stay away ever since."

It was getting hard for her to breathe. He was closer but still too damn far away. She ached for him to breach the inches between them and kiss her, touch her, do *something.*

"If I do this thing, if I come out as a wolf…" She swallowed thickly, forcing air into her lungs. "I'm going to need a friend."

His face clouded. "A friend. Not a lover."

"A friend…" Her breathing was definitely labored now. "And maybe a lover."

His eyes blazed at her words, but he still had a wild-eyed look to him—as if he was more afraid of kissing her than anything he'd done in his life. Her body trembled with need, but she was paralyzed by it. Then something broke in his expression, and before she could blink, he was on her—his hands in her hair and at the small of her back, crushing her to him; his mouth on hers, hungry and demanding; his rock-hard body pressed against the length of hers, overshadowing her, enveloping her, desiring her. The kiss was fast and breathless, and it felt like he was consuming her. It knocked her senseless, her arms limp at her side, engulfed by him.

It stopped as suddenly as it started.

He still held her, chest heaving into hers, but he pulled his lips from her bruised ones. She was on fire with need for him, which finally translated into her arms coming to life and gripping his massive shoulders, solid and heavy with muscles. He was so insanely *masculine*, raw strength under her hands, that the heated spot between her legs was instantly wet and aching.

He was breathing hard, barely two inches from her face. "Do you want to know my fantasy?"

Oh God, yes. She nodded, struck mute by the fact that this was happening. To her. In her bedroom.

"I picture you naked and beautiful in that field and…" He faltered, blinking… then he gave her that hungry look again. "And I dream of being the kind of man who actually deserves someone as innocent and beautiful as you. Then I want to kill anything that even threatens to harm you. And I remember that's what I truly am—a killer." His hold loosened on her. "You don't want someone like me for a lover, Grace. I'm broken."

No, no, no, her wolf protested. She gripped his shoulders, but he easily moved away from her.

She had no chance of holding him if he didn't want to be held.

And that felt like an avalanche crashing down on her heart.

Chapter Nine

There. He said it. No uncertain terms.

He was a killer. And a broken man at that.

She should run from him. Or at least push him away, just as his mate, Avery, had done. *No.* He couldn't think about that. But Grace wasn't doing any of those things... instead, her hands were still trying to hold him, only giving up when he stepped completely out of reach.

"You're not a bad man." She said it with fists clenched by her side, tears glassing her eyes.

But she didn't know. Or maybe she simply didn't believe him.

"I am, Grace."

"Jared—" She stopped herself, looking even more frustrated. "Is that even your name?" she demanded. She was starting to get angry, which speared something inside him. He expected it, but it was a blow all the same. And the pieces of him were threatening to come apart again.

"Yes," he said heavily. "Jared. Last name River. Not that it matters."

"It matters to me!" She stomped toward him on those small, delicate feet, and he found himself backing up in equal measure. As if he were actually afraid of her touch. Which he was—if she got any closer, he might give in to another of those scorching hot kisses. And then he would come completely undone. He could feel the threat of it pulling at the threads of his being—his sanity— with red-hot pinchers.

She reached him anyway, stopping just before touching him. "Jared River, you killed people in the war."

Her words stabbed straight into him. "Yes." It was becoming hard to breathe.

She was blinking rapidly, determination on her face. "You said you were a sharp-shooter. Which means you looked through your scope and saw their faces before you killed them."

He couldn't help wincing with the pain. "Yes."

"You did your duty." Her voice softened, but her eyes were drilling into him.

And he could finally see what she was doing. "It doesn't matter if it was my duty. It doesn't matter if it needed to be done, or if there were lives saved because of it. *None of that matters*, Grace."

She edged toward him. "All of it matters."

He shook his head, hands up, fending her off. "No. It doesn't. Because in the end, all that matters is what I've become. I'm a *thing*, Grace. A thing that knows how to kill. I've used every shifter sense I have, all the training the Marines gave me, and I used it to hunt *people*. And kill them. It used up everything that I have. Everything that I *am*. It's all I'm good for anymore." Avery had said as much to him. And even if she had never said a word, he would have still known the truth of it, deep inside. There was nothing left of him anymore.

The war had dug deep and emptied him out.

"That's obviously not true." She gestured between them, but he didn't know what she meant. "You're *here*, doing this, trying to convince me to do the right thing. What happened in the Marines... you did what you had to."

"That's no excuse." Now he was angry. Why couldn't she understand? Why wouldn't she just let it be? She should leave him to his frozenness, his hardened shell—it was the only thing that held him together.

"It's not an excuse—it's the truth." She edged even closer, dangerously close. Close enough to reach out and kiss, but he'd already done that, and it had almost destroyed him.

"You don't want me, Grace. I'm not good enough for you."

She shook her head, and the tears were coming back again. He hated seeing them, even as they baffled him.

"The truth is, I'm not good enough for *you*," she said. "You've served your country, doing something brave and dangerous, even as it tore you apart. You sacrificed everything inside you for a cause greater than yourself. You're brave and selfless in a way I can only wish I'll be, when my turn comes." The tears were sliding down her cheeks, and he could hardly stand it. His wolf—the one good and decent part of him still left—was howling at him, ready to tear him to shreds for not going to her. For not doing everything he could to wipe away those tears.

"Grace." He could hear the begging in it.

She closed the gap between them and reached up to wrap her arms around his neck. "I want you like I've never wanted any man in my life," she whispered.

She pressed her soft lips to his... and his body unlocked. He pulled her delicate form against him, all sweet softness and blueberries-and-cream scent filling his head. His mouth devoured hers, his wolf demanding even more. His hands were everywhere, skimming the thin lines and soft curves and delicious heat of her body. He lifted her from the floor, her small body melting into his, her toes barely kissing the floor as he carried her quickly backward to the bed. His wolf was howling to fulfill that fantasy of hers—throw her to the bed and ravish her body—but he hesitated, holding her while hovering at the edge of the mattress. If he made love to her, he couldn't possibly kill her father. And assassinating the Senator was something he might yet *have* to do. He couldn't have one without losing the other... but at this moment, he couldn't bear the thought of losing *her.* Because she was making him feel *alive*—dangerously, gloriously alive—and that might pull apart all the pieces of him... but there was nothing on earth he wanted more.

He kissed her again, rough and demanding, and carried her back onto the bed. Then he was covering her body with his—she was lost underneath him, squirming at his every touch, rocketing his erection to full strength in seconds. He lifted his mouth away from the demands he was making of hers long enough to rip open her blouse. The soft, silky fabric gave way under his fingers. She gasped, but it was filled with pleasure. He shifted one claw, just enough to slice free the front of her bra. Her eyes were wide now, her chest heaving, and those perfectly rounded breasts were calling to him with their tightly puckered nipples. He dove in, hands and mouth feasting upon them. She made a mewling sound, like a kitten, that went straight to his cock and turned his kneading of her breasts even more rough. He bit down on her tight nipples, making her cry out, and satisfaction coursed through him. He yearned to take her fast and hard. *Now.*

His need for her was so great, he almost didn't hear her words.

"Jared," she gasped. "Jared!"

He jerked back. "What?" His breath was heaving, but a cool spike of fear lanced through him. "Are you okay?" Not waiting for an answer, he scanned her body. Red marks were blossoming where his hold on her creamy white flesh had been too strong. "Oh God…" He lifted himself off her completely. "Grace... are you all right? Please tell me you're all right." The fear running through him —that he'd hurt her—turned every muscle to jelly. The only thing keeping him on the bed, next to her, was the desperate need to hear from her own lips that she was... that he hadn't...

She groaned and heaved up to sitting, then rolled closer to wrap her arms around his neck. Her skirt rode up as her leg hooked over his hip. It took him a second to realize that her groan was frustration, not pain.

"For God's sake, Jared... don't *stop.*" Her beautiful blue eyes blazed with heat as she stared into his, her panting breath washing over him. "I just had to tell you something first."

"Tell me something?" His hands had found her again without him even thinking about it, but they were holding her gently now. Skimming her back, gliding over her hip, but softly, softly... he didn't care what her fantasies were, he wasn't losing control like that again.

"I just... needed to tell you..." She was leaning into him, clenching her small hands on his shoulders to leverage closer. Her bare chest rubbed against the cotton of his shirt, and he ached to have her skin-to-skin. But he wasn't moving a muscle in that regard, not until she got out what she was trying to say.

He threaded one hand into her hair. "What is it, Grace?"

She swallowed and ducked her head, which meant she was staring at the point where their bodies touched. "It's just that this is my first time. So... you should probably know that."

"Your first...?" He pulled back. Did she mean... "You're a virgin?" He peered down at her, trying to catch her gaze. She wouldn't look at him. "Jesus, Grace! You don't want me to be your first—"

Her head whipped up. "Don't start with that again. I *absolutely* want you to be my first!"

"But... I..." His brow wrinkled up. "I'm sorry, Grace, but you're a gorgeous woman. You're smart and vivacious and... *alive*. Why..." But he stopped —because that wasn't the right question to ask.

The tight anger on her face told him he figured that out about five words too late.

"I'd like to see *you* try to have sex when you're the Senator's daughter and everyone watches your every move!" She was angry, but he could hear the hurt. She pushed away from him, falling back on the bed. "Not to mention that my damn wolf comes out every time I get..." She pressed her lips together, blushing furiously, sneaking a glance at him, then turning her back on him.

"Hang on, now." He reached for her, but by the time he pulled her back, tears were already leaking from the corners of her eyes. "I'm sorry, I didn't mean... I was just... *surprised*. What is this about your wolf?" He slid closer on the bed, drawing her against his body again. It sent a flood of relief through him, a melting feeling like he hadn't felt since... since Avery. But he shoved that thought aside, focusing on the tearful anger on Grace's face as she cuddled into him, head ducked, fingers playing with the buttons on his shirt. He bent to kiss the top of her head, inhaling the sweet fragrance of her beautiful hair. The knot she'd tied in the back was slightly askew from their brief tumble.

"Tell me about it, Grace," he said softly.

"It's not like I've never..." She swallowed.

He waited. His body was still dying to ravish hers, but he would wait forever for her to say what she needed to. And if this really *was* her first time... there was no way in hell he was rushing any part of it.

She laid a hand flat on his chest, over his thudding heart. "It's not like I've never climaxed before… if making love to my vibrator counts. But somehow that's different."

He smiled. "Well… I'm glad to hear that, actually."

One side of her mouth quirked up, and she snuck a look at him, then went back to staring at his chest. Her hands were in motion now, and it was driving him crazy.

"When I'm with a man," she whispered, "it's too intense. Too exciting. My wolf wants to come out."

"And you have a hard time controlling it in the first place."

Her eyes were soft and round when she looked up. "I didn't want you to be surprised, you know, in case I shifted in the middle of…" She swallowed. "I've never gotten very far with a man before. A few times… well, it just scared the hell out of me. I couldn't take the chance."

He nodded, and a warmth spread through him. He *was* going to be her first, and not just with sex. With the freedom to embrace who she really was. He leaned in to kiss her lightly on the lips, then pulled back, smiling. It was a strange feeling, this grin that she kept pulling out of him, but he couldn't help it.

"Most wolves have to learn how to control themselves early on, when they're teenagers," he said. "But you haven't had anyone to help you. Plus you've probably been trying to hold your wolf back most of the time." He ran his finger along the edge of her hair to the knot in back. "Don't worry. There's nothing you can do that will hurt me. Or surprise me."

"What if my claws come out?" Her breathing sped up a little as he started pulling pins from her hair, working the long spill of it loose.

His smile grew, both at the idea of having that gorgeous hair fisted in his hand as he made love to her and at the idea that she might be able to hurt him with her white-wolf kitten claws. He tipped her chin up to nibble at her neck. The delicious sound of her gasping breath came again. His heart hammered. He was going to do this—make love to her, help her embrace her wolf—even if it cracked him wide open and everything that he was tumbled out.

"Shifters have incredible healing powers," he whispered along her sweet, tender neck, then down further to her delicate collarbones. "Let your wolf loose, sweet Grace. I promise there's nothing you can do that wouldn't just turn me on even more."

She gasped as he laid a line of wet kissed down to her breast. "I don't... I don't want to hurt you." But her hands were deep in his hair, urging him on.

"Trust me," he said, taking a quick taste of her nipple. "Pain is *not* what I'm going to feel." He lifted her bottom so he could unzip and slide off her skirt. Her delicate, white panties were practically see-through with the wetness already gathered there. His mouth watered, and that unbalanced feeling came back—only he wasn't teetering on the precipice any longer. He had taken the leap and was free-falling down. He was going to make love to this gorgeous woman, and it would break him open. There was no going back, and most strange of all... he didn't want to.

He edged her panties down, gently at first, then ripping them with a slightly shifted claw just because he was impatient to have her. She sucked in a breath, watching him as he kissed a line across her sweet belly straight down to her sex.

"Jared." She said his name like a plea, so he picked up his pace. One hand cupping her deliciously tight breast, the other sliding along her thigh to open her up to him. When his tongue reached her sex, she gasped his name again and clutched his shoulders with both hands. She trembled underneath him, and he hardly had time to settle in and enjoy her before she was bucking her hips against him and moaning his name. She was already so wet, he stopped tormenting her nub just so he wouldn't get her there too quickly.

"Goddammit, Jared, don't you dare stop!" Her words were half gasps.

He just chuckled and thrust two fingers inside her, using his thumb to give her nub the attention it needed. She shrieked and bucked again. He lifted himself away from tasting her sex, running his tongue up the length of her body, tasting there instead. He was still fully clothed in his dress shirt and pants, and that needed to change. *Soon.* But for the moment, he was going to give Grace a hell of a warmup—he wanted her first time to blow away every other experience. She was panting when he reached her lips, so he just nibbled the side of her jaw. Her gorgeous hair was spilling all over her body as she bucked against him.

"Oh, God. Oh, God." She kept saying it over and over again, and he could feel her quivering, racing toward her climax. He slowed the thrust of his fingers slightly, deepening their reach and drawing it out for her. Her answering moan was almost as gratifying as the claws that came out and dug into his back, shredding his shirt.

He gritted his teeth, but the pain was just making his cock pulse. "Embrace your wolf," he whispered into her ear. "She's part of you. She wants this as much as you do. Give it to her. Let her enjoy it." Grace's moans turned into small cries, peaking with each thrust of his hand. *God,* he was aching to be inside her, to feel that quickening around his cock. Soon… very soon.

Her claws retracted back into fingers as she bucked even more strongly against him.

He feasted on her neck, hoping to bring it faster. "Come for me, Grace," he panted against her skin.

She cried out, grabbed onto his shoulders, and arched up from the bed. Her body clenched around his fingers, squeezing hard in an orgasm that rippled across her skin, making it shiver in the most delicious way possible. She called out his name at the height of it, and he felt her pleasure like it was his own, washing through him in warm waves.

The waves broke, and the seams came apart inside him. All the pieces and pain and frozen hardness he'd kept locked away were powerless against the satisfaction of giving this to Grace. Of being her first. Of earning her trust. Of bringing her together with her wolf.

He wanted to be inside her—and he would just as soon as she was ready—but she was already inside *him,* burrowing deep and shattering him hard.

She'd somehow found his heart and laid it bare.

He didn't know if he would be worth anything after this was done, but he was seeing all of it through, no matter what. He kissed her cheeks, her forehead, her sweet, sweet lips. Her body was flushed with the pleasure he'd given her, and he'd give her more—so much more—before he was done.

But she already owned every part of him.

Chapter Ten

GRACE WAS STILL SEEING STARS FROM THE LAST orgasm Jared gave her while he quickly tore off his white shirt and dress pants. The shoulders of the shirt were shredded from when her claws came out, but he just tossed it aside and quickly slid his deliciously hot, iron-muscled body on top of her again. She had already come harder than she ever had before, and the boy had been just using his hands and mouth. With that enormous cock of his poised at her entrance, and waves of pleasure still rippling through her, she was afraid she was going to hyperventilate before he could manage to take her... and become the first man she'd ever allowed inside her in that most intimate of ways.

He was waiting. Probably for her to stop

panting so hard in his face, which was gazing down at her with a soft expression that captured her heart.

"I want to be inside you, Grace," he whispered, soft lips against her cheeks, gently alternating kisses with words.

"Please, God, yes," she managed to get out.

She felt him smile against her skin, but her urgent grip on his massive, hard-muscled shoulders didn't make him move any closer to giving her what she wanted. Her fantasy before had been one of wanton sex with a hot man—now she just wanted Jared River inside her, connected to her, as close to her as she could hold this gorgeous, amazing man. The need wasn't even for *her* anymore—she had a sense that, as strong as he was, as good as his heart was, that this large, powerful man was *fragile*. That he needed her help. The wounds inside him had shut him down, closed him off from the world, and right now, at this moment... he was opening up. He needed her in a way that no one ever had. She wanted to give herself to him not just because he would take her to pleasure heights she'd never known... but because he needed that connection with the world again. Through *her*.

Tears stung the backs of her eyes. *God,* she was falling for him.

"Are you sure you're ready?" His voice was so gentle.

"I couldn't be any more ready." Her breathing was calming a little, and she felt less delirious than a moment before. Maybe that was why he was waiting, gently hovering above her, but not taking her.

He kissed her on the lips, just a soft brush. "I'm not in the habit of deflowering virgins." He glanced down, between their bodies, to where they were almost-but-not-quite-yet joined together. He eased a little closer, apply pressure to her entrance with his cock, but not entering.

She groaned. "Stop teasing me!"

"I'm not." But he grinned like he was. "But I *am* rather on the large side."

She grabbed his face and forced him to look into her eyes. "Why do you think I chose you? I didn't want just *anyone* for my first time. A girl has standards."

He chuckled, and his smile flushed a warmth through her that had nothing to do with his blazing hot body pressed against her, taunting her. Okay, maybe a little, but *dammit...* she really was falling for this man. This *shifter.*

His smile dimmed to seriousness. "I don't want to hurt you, Grace. I'll go slow. You tell me if you need me to stop, all right?"

She dug her fingers into his shoulders. "If I have coherent words, they're going to be of the form *don't stop, don't stop, don't stop.*"

He flashed a grin again, then it smoldered into a wicked look. "That's my plan, sweet Grace." But he *still* didn't enter her. Instead, he dropped his head down to give slow, nibbling kisses along her neck. She tilted her head for him, because *God*, that felt good. One of his hands held the weight of his body off hers, but the other was now roaming her, squeezing her breasts, toying with her nipples, then dipping down to brush her sex. His touch sent small electric shocks of pleasure through her—the circles he was drawing over her sex were quickly ramping her heart rate. Then his body started slowly rocking, and she felt the pressure of him easing inside her— one inch at a time, slowly stretching her, then retreating, forward then back. It was slow and hypnotic and intensely erotic as he teasingly filled her body with his. Her panting turned to moans, then to small cries as he took her.

"Oh, God, Jared," she managed to get out when he finally sunk all the way inside.

He stilled. "Am I hurting you?" His voice was hoarse, and she loved the sound of *need* inside it.

"No… just… *please* move!"

He groaned, pulled back, then pushed all the way into her in one swift stroke. She cried out with the shock and pleasure of it and clenched his shoulders tighter. He pulled back again and took her harder. Then harder. Each stroke was stronger than the last, and she clung to him like she was riding a hurricane, his body owning hers, possessing her with his groans and thrusts and body.

"Grace, you're so damn tight," he said as he thrust into her again. "I can't… baby, come for me!"

She couldn't even respond—she just whimpered as her pleasure grew stronger with each pound. He shifted position, pulling away, lifting her hips, and angling deeper—she shrieked as he plunged into her again, reaching farther than he had before. His hand slipped down to her nub as he thrust into her again and again. A scream erupted from her lips as that extra touch hurtled her right over the edge. Her body bucked furiously against him, wave after wave of pleasure possessing her like the most delicious of demons. He was still thrusting through it all, and just as she thought she couldn't feel anything more, he slammed deep and held, groaning and growling in pleasure. She could feel his cock twitching inside her, pumping out his release.

Then he collapsed down on top of her, his body pressing against hers, still buried inside her. Leftover shock waves were twitching his body. She held onto him fiercely. She'd never felt anything like this—not just the pleasure, but the intimacy. The utter completeness of sharing everything she was with another person. The warmth that suffused her wasn't just afterglow… it was very much like love.

How had she fallen so fast and so hard for this man she barely knew?

But that wasn't the truth—she knew everything she needed to know about Jared River. Even in these hot, sticky moments just after they'd both climaxed, he was showing the kind of man he was —gently kissing her and asking if she was all right; carefully keeping his massive weight off her body while lavishing attention on it with his hands and mouth and hot, hot gaze; even the tender way he eased down to the bed next to her and brushed a tendril of hair from her face. All of it spoke of the man who was claiming her heart.

"You're so beautiful, Grace," he whispered,

ALISA WOODS

reverently, and her heart filled to overflowing. If she could have this man, even once, her life would never be the same. If she could hold onto him for longer... but she tried not to think of that, for the moment. This was just one time, one act, and there were so many unknowns lying ahead. She couldn't know what the future held, not yet.

She turned to face him on the bed, both of them lying on their sides. She touched the slight stubble growing on his cheek. His smile in return made her glow inside. Then she realized...

"My wolf didn't come out this time," she said with awe.

His eyes sparkled. "Because you're not fighting her anymore."

He was right. Her wolf was humming with the pleasure they'd both had at the hands of their alpha. Wait... what? Her eyes widened, and she peered into his. "Are you an alpha wolf?"

His eyebrows hiked up, but his arms snuggled her closer. "I haven't been anyone's alpha in a long time. Why do you ask?"

"I'm not even sure what an alpha wolf is, not really." She bit her lip. "But my wolf is saying you're my alpha."

The expression on his face morphed from

142

surprise to an inscrutable expression so intense, it made her heart quiver. "Is that bad?" she asked, afraid she'd said the wrong thing.

"No." It was a whisper. He pulled her in for a gentle kiss on her forehead, then he cleared his throat. "An alpha is the dominant wolf of a pack. Or a mating pair. Your wolf is saying... she's saying she wants me to claim you." His voice trembled, just slightly, and her arms automatically went out to hug him, hold him, beat back whatever was causing this torrent of emotion to run through him. She imagined he had locked away all his feelings for so long, and if he was anything like her at the moment, he was inundated with them. His large hands fanned across her back, holding her tight.

When they loosened, she pulled back to look into his eyes. "There's so much I don't know, but I don't want you to explain if it's going to... hurt you in some way."

"It's all right." He cupped a hand against her cheek. "Although I will say that having you naked next to me makes pretty much anything bearable."

She smiled, and her heart did that swelling thing again. Then she gave him a bashful look. "What does it mean to claim someone?" she asked softly. "Did we... I mean, we only made love, right?

But it was incredible. Was that you… *claiming* me?" She shivered slightly at the word, and her wolf was back to panting and wanting Jared between her legs again. The sound of it was so… possessive and *male* and hot. Whatever it was, she was up for trying it.

She must be way off base because he just grinned. Not unkindly, but it made her duck her head, her cheeks heating with embarrassment.

"Hey," he said softly, lifting her chin with a finger to peer into her eyes. "Never be ashamed to ask me anything, okay?"

She nodded. There was so much she didn't know, she couldn't afford to be embarrassed by that —not if she was going to embrace this shifter thing and live in their world. Because that was the leap she had already taken.

He stroked the long length of her hair spilling over her shoulders. "Claiming is the most intense sexual experience a wolf can have." He grinned as her eyebrows lifted. "But it's really much more than that. When a wolf mates, the female pledges her submission to the male, and—"

"Wait, what? Submission? Is that some kind of kinky thing?"

He laughed—the strength of his large chest

heaving shook her entire bed, bouncing her along with it.

"Okay, okay," she said, clinging to him, so he wouldn't edge away with the shaking. "So, I'm clueless. I'll shut up now and let you explain."

He tamed the laughter then quickly rolled her on her back, pinning her to the bed and kissing her. When he let her breathe again, he said, "The only time I want you to shut up, Grace Krepky, is when your mouth is on mine. Or other parts of me."

A warm gush of heat flooded her swollen and sore nether parts. *Holy Christ,* what would it be like to go down on Jared River? Her mouth watered just at the thought of it.

"What were we talking about, again?" she asked. "I'm feeling the need to have other parts of you in my mouth." She gave him a dead serious look.

His eyes hooded. "You have no idea what that's doing to me."

"Let's find out." She licked her lips, hungry for him.

He groaned and rolled off her, but then drew her close again, cuddling. "Sweet Grace, we've already spent too much time alone in your room. We'll have to get dressed soon. And wash the sex off us. Human ability to scent isn't as strong, but it would take an idiot not to realize what we've been doing. And your father's not an idiot."

Her father. *Right.* She was going to need to tell him about all of this… at least the part where she was a shifter. But she had to make a plan before rushing into that. And before she could make a plan, she needed to know more about wolves.

She tried to put on a serious face and ignore the fact that an extremely hot shifter was lying naked in bed next to her. And that she wanted to have sex with him, many different ways, again and again. As soon as possible. "All right. Back to business. Tell me about this claiming thing. And I have other questions after that, but I'll try not to interrupt."

His smile was warm. "All right. Let's start with submission. Any wolf can submit to an alpha—either as part of a pack or a mating. It's a magical bond that ties them together: the alpha pledges to protect their pack or their mate, and wolves who submit are pledging their obedience."

"Obedience," she said coolly. "That sounds… yeah, I'm going with *kinky* again."

He tapped her nose with his finger. "It's not like that. The pledge strengthens the alpha in a literal, magical sense. When the alpha is stronger, the pack is stronger. Or the mate pair, including their pups. And the alpha would never hurt those who have submitted to him. It's really in everyone's interest, and it feels... amazing. You'll have to experience it to see. For mated pairs, it starts with submission, but it goes beyond that. Once the female submits, they make love. And during the act..." He trailed a finger along her jaw, drawing a hot line down to the crook of her neck. "He bites her." He leaned in and nipped deliciously at her neck.

She couldn't help sucking in a hot breath.

The grin on his face was wide when he pulled back.

She swallowed. "Okay, that's hot even when you're not actually biting me."

He licked his lips. "You have no idea, sweet Grace. When the male claims his mate with his bite and his love, his magic flows into her. The pleasure is like nothing you've ever experienced." His face shadowed, and he suddenly grew quiet.

Her eyes went wide as she remembered. "You had a mate once," she said softly.

His expression locked down. "She's dead now."

"I'm sorry." She bit her lip, unsure if she should say anything more. But she couldn't help herself—because she was falling in love with this hot, sexy shifter. "Can you have more than one mate? I mean… is it a one-time thing?" God, she hoped not. She wasn't even sure what it meant to submit, much less be mated—was that for life?—but she needed to understood at least what the possibilities were, especially between her and Jared.

He hesitated, his gaze lowered, not meeting hers. "No, I could have another mate." He raised his eyes to meet hers. "I just never thought I would."

"You don't have to tell me about her," she whispered with a shake of her head, all while thinking, *please tell me about her.* This felt important—it seemed like part of what drove Jared to lock himself down. And Grace knew that *she* was part of what was opening him up again. She couldn't do that—she couldn't help him overcome his past—if she didn't even know what it was that shut him down in the first place.

He held her gaze, but his eyes weren't hard and his expression wasn't that stone-faced look he'd worn so many times. "Her name was Avery," he said, finally. Then he sucked in a deep breath.

She reached a hand to press flat against his chest, over his heart. He glanced at her hand and placed his over it, holding her to him, then looking up into her eyes again. "I like it when you do that."

She smiled a little and waited to see if he would share more.

"I mated before I went overseas to serve," he said quietly. "When I came back... I was different. Avery sensed it. She asked what had happened, and I told her, and..." He swallowed, and dropped his gaze again, avoiding hers. "She was horrified. Repulsed by it. I don't blame her, not really. War is horrifying. She pulled away, and I didn't have anything left in me to keep her. I was already dead inside—the war had done that to me. I couldn't leave it behind, even though I was back home. I never really knew if that was what drove her away —not what I'd done, but who it made me become. In the end, it didn't really matter." He dropped his gaze to his hand holding hers against his chest. "When she left me, I had nothing but the war inside. So I re-enlisted, did another tour. While I was gone, she died. Simple car accident. Happens every day. I wasn't there to protect her. Maybe I couldn't have done anything, but I'll never know."

She cupped his cheek with her hand, tears threatening her eyes. "I'm so sorry."

He looked up, eyes glassy with tears that

weren't being shed. "When I lost her—my mate—I lost *everything.* I lost *myself.* Being alone and isolated is the worst thing that can happen to a wolf. It's not *supposed* to happen. I still had my brothers and my pack, but I pulled away from them all. I've been dead inside for so long… and then I saw *you.*" He gave her a smile that seemed pained. "You were isolated, a wolf in hiding, and my wolf… he took one look at you, and he sent me tearing off into the woods to protect you. Because no one should be alone like that. No one."

The tears were flowing down her face now. "Jared." She didn't know what to do, how to say the feelings that were bursting inside her, so she pulled him closer and kissed him, long and hard and hungry. "I'm not alone," she said when she paused for breath. "I have you."

He pressed his forehead to hers. "Protecting you is the best thing I've done in a long time."

She searched his eyes. "I want more than just your protection."

He smiled. "The lovemaking comes included. Package deal."

She smirked and blinked away her tears. Then her gaze fell on their hands still clasped over his heart. "I want even more than that." She pulled her gaze up to his eyes.

All humor had fled his face.

She touched his cheek with her fingertips. "I want you for my mate."

"Oh, Grace." Her words seemed to pain him.

"I know it's fast, and I don't even really understand, and this is all so crazy, but—"

He cut her off by rolling her on her back again and pinning her with his hot, sexy, naked body. "Shhhh…" Then he smothered her words with a kiss. "Don't say it. Don't say those words… not until I can do something about them." Then he erased all doubt by nipping a line of small tastes down on her neck—just with human teeth, but it ran shivers of pleasure up and down her body. Her wolf howled in triumph. Grace was light-headed with panting by the time he raised his head from her flesh again.

"I want you so badly, Grace." His breath was hot on her face. Before she could say *Yes!* he pulled back and said, "But we really can't do this now."

She willed her heart to stop pounding so hard. "No, you're right. We need to… think. And not just have sex like crazed teenagers."

He just chuckled and rolled away from her,

rubbing his face hard and blowing out a deep breath. "Rain check for lovemaking at a later time."

"Hell yes."

He grinned at her, then gave her a serious look. "What's your plan with this, Grace?"

She forced herself to sit up in the bed. That was the only way she wouldn't simply throw herself at him again. "Shower. Fresh clothes." She turned to face him. "Then a strategy to destroy my father's anti-shifter legislation."

His face went solemn, and he just nodded.

Grace took a deep breath and prepared to start the rest of her life.

As a shifter.

Chapter Eleven

Night had fallen on his family's safehouse.

Jared had been gone less than a day, but it had been a life-changing twenty-four hours. He pulled his car into the large, graveled parking lot—it was filled to capacity with all the shifters who were staying with them now. His family's estate was large, but it was stuffed to the rafters with all the shifters who had been rescued from Agent Smith's medical prison—and the experiments fully authorized by Senator Krepky. At least, that was their operational theory, even though they didn't have definitive proof of the connection. And barring some smoking-gun evidence, Grace would be the key to bringing the Senator down—she'd embraced that fact, he was certain, but she needed time to act on it. Which meant waiting until the morning.

He hated leaving her in that house with her father—his stomach had been chewing itself into pieces ever since he left—but even as her personal bodyguard, he had no plausible reason to stay there overnight. Garrison Allied's normal security was supposedly sufficient to keep the Senator and his daughter safe while ensconced in their estate. It was probably just as well—any more time in her presence, especially in her bedroom, and Jared would've been making love to her again and again. They had managed to get away with it so far, and soon enough she would be telling her father she was a shifter—after that, Jared would be free to spend as much time with her as he and his wolf could handle. At least, that was *his* plan... assuming she would still want him.

But just being separated for the night was killing him.

The plan was for her to come out to her father tomorrow morning and threaten to take it public if he didn't back down on his legislation. Apparently, she and her father had some kind of strategy meeting in the mornings before they headed off for the day's schedule of campaign activities. Jared would be back at the estate bright and early in the morning, standing by her side as she told her father she was a wolf. Grace claimed this was the best approach, the best way to bring down her father's plans, and as nervous as it made him, he trusted her. In the meantime, he needed to report back to his brothers and make sure they were on board with the plan and not moving on some separate front without him.

Jared strolled in the front door of the safehouse. The great room was bustling with people he didn't know, and the scent of dinner lingered in the air even though the dining room had been cleared out. He didn't see his brothers among the meandering and chattering temporary residents of his home, but he caught a glimpse of his mother's long gray hair as she disappeared into the kitchen.

He strode after her. She had three shifters on kitchen duty, cleaning up the massive pile of dishes left over from the evening's meal. They weren't letting her lift a finger and had set up some kind of production line to get the job done, but she was definitely in charge.

"That bowl goes on the top shelf, Owen," she said. Owen was ex-military, one of Jace's brothers-in-arms, and he'd been a prisoner of Agent Smith's for over a year. The guy looked like shit when they first rescued him, a few days ago, but some of the black circles under his eyes had already started to disappear with Mama River's good cooking and attentive care. She mothered everyone, whether they needed it or not... but most of them did.

"Yes, Ma'am," Owen said with a small smile and a nod for Jared behind her. Owen quickly stowed the bowl on the top shelf and returned to his station at the end of the production line of washing, drying, and putting away the dishes.

Jared's mother turned to him. "You missed dinner." Her small scowl was more a concern that he hadn't eaten at all, not that he had missed her particular spread that night. His mother could support the 10th Mountain Division on KP duty, if she had to. One missing shifter from the table wouldn't alarm her.

He stepped forward and dropped a quick kiss on her cheek. She startled, eyes wide, and he smiled as a blush crept up on her cheeks.

"Don't think that's going to earn you forgiveness." But her voice faltered a little.

He just grinned wider—he hadn't done anything like that in forever. But a painfully wrenching sense of hope and life stirred inside him, and it was no mystery why—Grace had brought him back, almost literally, from the dead.

"You could put me on KP duty as punishment," he suggested.

His smile was still throwing her. "Shut up and sit down," she ordered, gesturing to the small table in the corner of the kitchen. "I'll rustle up some leftovers." She swept toward the massive refrigerator where she kept her supplies to feed the hungry hordes.

He could tell she wanted to say something, but there were way too many people present. Fellow shifters, but still strangers. Not even pack, much less family. She dug around in the refrigerator and came out with bread, an assortment of sandwich meats, and condiments. He relieved her of the jumbled mix and carried them to the table.

She turned to her KP detail. "You can just leave the rest of that." She waved them away from the sink.

Owen frowned. "We're not letting you touch a bit of this mess, Mama River. You best get used to that." His Texas drawl was no match for his mama's will.

Jared took a seat at the table and just folded his hands behind his head to watch.

His mother parked her delicate hands on her hips and gave Owen her patented glare. "Private First Class Owen Harding, I need you to *clear the room,* soldier. You can finish kitchen duty when I'm good and ready for you to."

The other shifters turned to send a questioning look her way. Owen hiked up his eyebrows, but then glanced at Jared and seemed to figure it out.

"You heard the lady," Owen said barked to the others. *"Clear out."* As the lot of them trotted out of the room, Owen said quietly as he passed her, "You touch any of those dishes, Mama River, and we're going to have a talk about the proper meaning of gratitude."

She shook her finger at him on his way out. "Don't you sass me, Owen Harding. You haven't earned that privilege yet."

He just grinned as he left the room.

His mother came and sat with him. "Jared Anthony River, you tell me right now what's happened."

"I thought you wanted me to eat," he teased, gesturing to all the sandwich fixings.

"This is the one time you can eat while talking at the same time." Her serious expression didn't waver.

He shook his head, rueful that a couple smiles and a kiss on the cheek was grounds for this level of concern in his mother. He'd been way too deep in his own head for too long. The toll it had taken on his family was becoming painfully obvious.

"I'm good, Mama," he said softly. "I know I've been... distant. Hell, let's just say it—I've been broken. I know that's worried you, and I'm sorry for that."

She grasped onto his forearm, which was lying on the table. "You've got nothing to be sorry for. Not then, and not now. Full stop."

She was talking about Avery. And the war. It was no secret, at least among his family, what had happened with all of it. "It's not that, Mama. I met someone, and she's..." Gorgeous. Sexy. Bringing him to life in a way that caused a smile to break out on his face at the slightest provocation. "She's something special."

If the word *joy* had been stamped on his mother's forehead, it wouldn't have been any more obvious how she felt. That look settled something deep inside him—something that Grace stirred up and revived. And now she was bringing healing to not just him, but to the people he loved.

Tears pricked his eyes—which flat astounded him. They vanished in his surprise.

The smile lines around his mother's eyes crinkled. "When do I get to meet this girl?"

Jared smiled again. He loved this most about his mother—complete and total acceptance of people. No judgment. Just joy.

"Soon, I hope. She's in a bit of trouble right now, and I aim to get her out of it." He glanced back at the open door to the dining room where several of the kitchen duty shifters were still lingering, pretending they weren't listening in. "Where are my brothers? I'm going to need their help."

She squeezed his arm where her hand rested, then let him go. "They're out back, fixing up some of the cabins. Making a home for their new mates. Maybe we need to make room for one more?"

His smile tempered, but his heart leapt—which made him realize just how much he wanted that. When Grace had said it, he thought his heart might burst with need. But he didn't want to get his mother's hopes up. Or his.

He shook his head. "I don't know, Mama. Can't rush her too much. She's in a fragile state right now. She needs me to go slow."

His mother nodded, just once, then stood up. "I

know you, son. You'll do what's best for her. No doubt in my mind about that." Then she gave him a slightly skeptical look—like she had reason to doubt he would do the best thing for *him*. That didn't concern him.

He rose up as well and hastily put together a sandwich. His mother nodded approvingly. Then he stuffed the sandwich in his face and chewed as he strode out to the back part of the estate. He was actually famished, so it went down quick.

They had horses and a few livestock in the stables, and the rich smell assaulted his nose, mixing with the pine scent that swept in from the forest behind the estate. This had always been home to him, even after he had moved out to the city like his brothers. And when he'd taken Avery for a mate, they'd used one of the bridal suites out back—a small, cozy cabin, just the two of them. It felt strange to even contemplate bringing Grace here, but this was his home. And she needed one—or at least, she would, once her father disowned her. That was the most likely outcome, and he wanted to have a place for her to come and feel welcome. He should bury the ghost of Avery now, once and for all, before Grace arrived. He didn't want her feeling even a hint of that lingering.

The animals were quiet, and there wasn't much activity out back, now that night had fallen. Light shone from two side-by-side cabins at the end of the row, and Jared figured that must be where his brothers, Jaxson and Jace, were making their new homes. As Jared approached the cabins, Jaxson strolled out of one, carrying three stacked boards on his shoulder.

"Hey, you're back," his brother said. "How's it going on the political front?"

Jared tipped his head to the second cabin—the front door was closed, but light poured from the windows. "Is Jace in there?"

"Yeah, we're trying to get stuff set up for a week from Saturday."

The two of them headed for the door. "What's happening then?" Jared asked.

"The weddings?" Jaxson smirked. "You didn't think our mother was going to let any grass grow under her feet with that, did you?"

No, he supposed not. Jared returned his smile.

Just like their mother, Jaxson startled at seeing Jared's grin. "What's going on?" he asked, stopping dead in his tracks.

Jared kept walking toward the cabin door. "I need to talk to you and Jace both."

Even before Jared open the door, he could hear the voices inside.

"Well, we can't fill the entire wall with shelving." That was his brother, Jace.

"Why not? It's the perfect corner for reading." Piper's voice had a little edge to it.

Jared opened the door just as Jace responded, "Because then we won't have room for the crib." He followed it up with a sexy smile, and Jace's arms wrapped around Piper's waist. His brother was going in for a kiss, and she was giving him a dead-sexy, encouraging smile.

Jared cleared his throat, and they both jumped. He smiled at them. "Hate to interrupt your baby-making plans, but I need a minute of your time."

Piper glared at him. "Jared, your timing *sucks.*"

He just laughed. "People have said much worse things about me."

Jace just stared at him with open-mouthed wonder, then he said to Jaxson, "What the hell happened to him?"

Apparently, the changes Grace had wrought in him were that obvious.

Jaxson brushed past him on his way into the cabin, then set down the shelving boards. "I don't

163

know, but I like the new Jared a lot better than the old Jared."

Piper was studying him with a gleam in her eye. "This is about the girl, isn't it?"

"Yeah." Jared closed the door behind him, then turned to their expectant faces. "Here's the thing: she's willing to come out to her father as a wolf. She thinks it will embarrass him, but even more important, she thinks she can use it to talk him out of the legislation. Make some argument about not putting her under the scrutiny of the law or some such thing."

Jaxson looked skeptical. "But you don't think it will work?"

Jared folded his arms. "She wants to appeal his sense of decency. I'm not entirely convinced the man has one. You should've seen his supporters at this anti-shifter rally today."

"I heard about that on the news," Jace said, releasing his hold on his new mate. "Something about a shifter gang crashing the rally and making threats?"

"That was all a setup." Jared shook his head. "The Senator orchestrated the whole thing."

"That's… disturbing." Jaxson rubbed the stubble on his chin, thoughtfully.

Jared nodded. "Grace saw right through it. And I told her about the experiments. I think she believes me, but she still wants a chance to talk her father out of the legislation. So we're waiting until morning. I came back here to check in and find out where you were with your side of things."

"Well, Olivia's got everything ready to roll out to the press," Jaxson said. "She's got shifters lined up to talk about it on camera, and she's alerted her friends in the media that she might be calling a press conference. She's just waiting for us to give her the word."

Jared nodded. "I just need a little more time. I don't want to throw Grace and her father under the bus with a press conference. Especially if we don't have any more evidence connecting him to the experiments. That might just force his hand into something more drastic."

"We do have *something* on him," Piper said. "I tapped a hacker—someone Olivia knew—to breach the Senate's email server. Got a raft of documents to sort through. But I've already found a couple emails between him and some guy named David Alcore. We think it might Agent Smith. There's probably more, once we dig through it all. Got several shifters working on it."

Jared sucked in a breath. "That's good news. And if we've got evidence against the Senator, we'll use it. But I trust Grace to help us—she wants to stop him as badly as we do."

Jace and Jaxson exchanged a look of concern. "Are you sure about that?" Jace asked. "This is her father we're talking about. She might not be willing to do what it takes to bring him down."

"I trust her." That was one thing Jared was sure about. "But I know she's emotionally compromised in this situation. She needs my help to get through it."

Piper's eyebrows lifted, and Jace and Jaxson looked surprised as well.

"So… sounds like *she* trusts *you.*" Piper nodded approvingly. "You're more than just her bodyguard now, aren't you?"

That he could feel at all defensive about that surprised him. "I'm not going to let her get hurt. She knows that. And I'm helping her, well, to explore her wolf side."

Jaxson broke out into a grin. "*Damn,* Jared. Sounds like you've been busy."

Shockingly, this made heat rise in his face. "We've been getting to know each other." He wasn't going to tell them all the details—they could figure that out for themselves—but they needed to know she was something special.

Jace shook his head. "Are you sure about this? She could be playing you, Jared."

That flared his wolf—his brother was talking about his mate. *His mate.* No, she wasn't that. Not yet. Maybe not ever. Still… he glowered at Jace. "If you'd met her, you'd realize that she's not playing anyone. She's not the type."

Jace looked unconvinced. "She's the Senator's campaign manager. She runs political campaigns *all the time*, Jared. And she's his daughter. She has all kinds of motivation to play you, and play you *hard*. I just don't want…" He exchanged another look with Jaxson. The smile fell off Jaxson's face. Even Piper looked concerned now. Jace turned back to him. "I just don't want you to get hurt," he finished.

Jared understood—he'd been broken for so long, it was a wonder they hadn't locked him up somewhere for his own good. "Grace would never hurt me. You'll have to trust me on this. And if she can't convince her father to stop the legislation, she's going to come out as a shifter and shut him down that way. She's been trying to stop him, even before she met me—before she really embraced what she was. The girl's been living with her secret for years. Denying it. She's just now owning it, and she's about to turn her whole world upside down to do the right thing. *She's* the one in danger of getting hurt here. And I'm not going to let that happen."

Jace's eyes were wide, but he was nodding now. "Alrighty, then." He and Jaxson exchanged a look of agreement. "We'll see what Grace can do first, before we do anything."

Piper's eyes were appraising him again. "You're her link to the shifter world."

Jared nodded. "She needs to know she can depend on me. In the morning, I'll be by her side when she tells her father. Just in case anything goes sideways."

"What do you need from us?" Jaxson asked, his face open and supportive.

Relief flushed through him. Jaxson was alpha, and no matter what doubts anyone else in the pack had, they would follow his lead. "I need you to hold tight until you hear from me again. It won't be long. Deal?"

They all nodded in agreement. Jared gave them a few more tight smiles, leaving them with grins on their faces as they finished preparations for their impending nuptials.

He didn't know how he would get through the

night—there likely wouldn't be any sleep for him. He should go for a run in the forest, burn off his energy and anxiety. His brothers were preparing for their new lives with their new mates—even with everything going on, they were filled with hope for the future. Piper and Jace were already getting busy on providing him with a little niece or nephew. That clutched at his heart, moving it in a way that felt like he was dying… or perhaps coming back to life.

For the first time in forever, it felt like he might have hope for the future as well.

Chapter Twelve

GRACE SLOWLY BUTTONED HER PALE-PINK SILK blouse, then smoothed down her pencil-thin black skirt. She gazed in the mirror, making sure all the tendrils of her hair were tucked neatly into the bun at the nape of her neck, like her father wished.

It was time to change her life.

This was a long time coming—she finally realized she had been waiting for something to come along and force her shifter issue out into the open. Her lady parts were happily sore from yesterday's encounter with Jared's cock, but she knew that having sex with him went way beyond just punching her V-card. Jared had rolled into her life like a thunderstorm and completely taken it over—and he was forcing the True Grace to come out. She finally felt

like the 25-year-old woman she wanted to be—
someone who could live comfortably inside her own
skin, embrace her inner wolf, and love a man with
such abandon that it left her lightheaded and thor-
oughly connected to him.

It was time she straightened out the rest of her
life, too—including the part where she vehemently
disagreed with her father on shifter policy. It was
way overdue for her to stand up and declare she
would no longer accept his bigoted opinions, much
less encourage them by being his campaign
manager. If she were lucky, she would still be able
to keep her world intact and bring her father
around to the righteous side of things. But she
honestly didn't expect that to happen. More likely,
her father would toss her out of the estate on her
ear. She would be out of a job, out of a home, and
without a family.

But she would have her dignity and integrity—
and that was way more important than all the rest.

If she were very lucky, she would have Jared as
well. She was uncertain at best about that—he had
been open and honest from the beginning about his
purpose in all this. He wanted to force her shifter
nature out into the open. He came to show her the
shifter side of things, and he certainly accomplished

that. But she didn't think she imagined the connection between them—or the sweet, sweet lovemaking that went far beyond the wildest, most powerful orgasm she'd ever had.

She had a feeling it was life-changing for both of them. Even more, she wanted to make sure Jared continued to open his heart to the world. To *live* again. That was almost as important to her as her own integrity—which she would be testing this morning.

A light tap on the door signaled Jared had arrived. She'd asked him to come and get her as soon as he reached the estate this morning.

She hurried over to the door and opened it. Glancing around and finding no one in the hall, she whispered, "I'd really like to kiss you Good Morning, but I don't think we should take the chance. Rain check?"

He smiled broadly, but kept his hands clasped in front of him, standing in a position of quiet power and authority. "We're taking enough chances this morning as it is."

She returned the smile. "I'd also like to tell you all the other things I want to do, but we have an appointment with my father."

Jared smile dimmed. "Are you ready for this?"

"I couldn't be any more ready." She smirked—that was the exact thing she had said before he took her virginity last night.

A sly smile crept onto his face. "I've hardly slept. Too busy thinking about you."

He was getting her hot and bothered, and that wouldn't do—they had things to accomplish first. She shook her finger at him as she stepped out of her room and closed the door behind her.

"No dirty talk, Jared River. I need to keep my professional face on."

His smirk grew even hotter. "That's really unfortunate." Then his smile tempered a little. "Grace, I'll be right by your side the whole time. No matter how this goes, I'm going to be there for you."

She drew in a deep breath as some of the nerves from earlier in the morning returned to flutter her stomach. "Let's do this."

She brushed past him, striding down the hallway, her heels clicking on the marble flooring. Jared followed. He was dressed in the same outfit as yesterday—dark blue jacket and pants and a starched white collared shirt. She had shredded the last shirt during their lovemaking, so this must be a new one.

When she reached her father's office, she held

her head high and marched in like it was just any other morning debriefing. She had the Senator's calendar ready, but she wanted to dive into the real reason she was here right away. No more time to waste.

Her father stood at his desk, peering down at his tablet. "Ah, Grace, good morning. I wanted to talk to you about this newscast today. I think we need a different host, or possibly a different show entirely. This person's just going to softball me with questions about the budget. And I want to use this to warm up to the shifter legislation for next week."

Well, this was her chance… queued up like he knew it was coming. "I'm sorry, I can't do that, Dad."

Her father looked up sharply. "Excuse me?" He flicked a quick look at Jared, but his gaze didn't even hesitate a moment there, just returned to Grace. "Is there some reason why this particular reporter is important to us? I thought it was just the local news."

He was always looking for the political advantage… not that she was any different. She understood this part of him—he had trained her well.

"It's not the reporter," Grace said. "It's the topic."

Her father frowned and lifted his finger from the tablet, then came around the desk, leaned back against it, and folded his arms. "Is this about the rally yesterday?"

"Yes." She took a breath, the words at the tip of her tongue, struggling to find a way to come out. "I need to talk to you about that."

The Senator sighed. "I know the shifter gang attack was unsettling, but this is exactly what I'm talking about, Grace. These people are dangerous, and they need to be identified for the common good. That's all I'm trying to accomplish with the legislation. But you *saw* the anger and fear out there in our constituency. We need to listen to that."

"No, we don't." Her passion about this was rising up. "We need to fight back against it, not pander to it. Part of leadership is showing the people they don't have to fear the things that frighten them."

The Senator's arms unfolded, and his fists clenched at his side. "We've been over and over this, Grace. I thought we were done with this stupid arguing. We're launching next week, for God's sake."

"No, we're not—at least, I'm not. Father, there's something you need to tell you—"

She was cut off by a knock at the Senator's door. She snapped her teeth together. Red fury had risen up in her father's face, but he held up an abrupt hand to stop her.

"Come!" he called out to whoever was at the door.

It creaked open, and the front guard, Richard, poked his head in. "Senator, there's a Robert Sanders here to see you, sir."

Her father gave a quick nod. "Send him in." Once Richard retreated, her father turned back to her. "Whatever you have to say, Grace, hold it until we're finished with this business. Perhaps it will illuminate your understanding a little better about the situation we're in."

Grace grimaced, wishing she had just forced the words out or could think of a way to put off this Robert Sanders person, but the sound of hard-soled shoes was already pounding on the marble flooring outside her father's office. She snuck a look at Jared, and he gave her a minuscule nod.

They could wait a few more minutes.

When the door opened, a tall, slender man strode in, wearing an ill-fitting suit but full of confidence. He moved with the kind of controlled power that reminded her of her father. "Good morning, Senator."

Her father was back at his desk, poking at his tablet. He waved in Grace's general direction. "Sanders, is my daughter, Grace." He looked up with a serious expression on his face. "I think it's time we read her in on everything."

Sanders turned to her, a skeptical look on his face. He opened his mouth to say something but cut off when he caught sight of Jared behind her.

"What the—" But then he didn't bother with words, he just reached into his jacket. Before Grace could even react, a blur of fur flashed past her.

Jared had shifted. Grace gasped, but before she could blink, Sanders had pulled a gun. Three shots banged through her father's office, piercing her eardrums and stopping her heart.

She screamed, her hands flying up against her mouth. *Jared had dropped like a stone.* He landed on the floor in front of her, a massive hulk of fur.

No, no, no. "What have you *done?*" Her legs felt weak. Her father hurried around the desk and skittered to a stop in front of Jared's body. She wanted to go to Jared, but the man still had his gun pointed at Jared's head.

"*No!*" Her father held up his hand to Sanders.

177

"What are you *doing?* I can't have dead bodies in my office!"

Sanders hesitated, but Jared started to move, struggling to rise up from the floor. The man gave him a swift kick. His shiny black shoes came away bloody.

"Oh, God," Grace sobbed, but she was frozen in place. Sanders quickly holstered his gun and pulled out another one. He pulled the trigger three times in rapid succession, but instead of bullets, it left darts sticking out of Jared's fur coat.

He slumped to the floor and stayed down.

A shiver grabbed hold of Grace and convulsed her from head to toe. Her wolf screamed in protest, wanting to come out to protect her alpha. But it was too late. Jared's gun lay on the floor, dropped along with his clothes. She wanted to pick it up, but she wouldn't even know how to use it.

"How could you?" Grace shouted at both men.

Her father stared at Jared's body. "How did you know?" he calmly asked Sanders, who was putting away his tranq gun.

"That is Jared River," he said coolly. "I had him in custody once. He's one of the River brothers that have been causing such trouble for us."

"These animals are *everywhere,"* her father said in

disgust. "Do you see what I mean, Grace? They're trying to *kill* us. They're criminals and spies. And apparently that threat against your life was all too real. Get Richard in here! I want to know how this happened. I want to know how a shifter ended up being a bodyguard for my daughter!"

Grace's hands shook, so she clenched them at her sides. Her body finally unlocked, and she stumbled to the floor, falling to her knees next to Jared, tears spilling. Her fingers automatically buried in his fur. "He's not a criminal! He's a *man*... a *good* man." The pain and anger and fear washed over her—she couldn't even tell if he was alive.

"Grace, get away from that animal!" her father yelled, reaching to haul her up from the floor.

She yanked away from him, scrambling backward. A shiver ran down her again from head to foot, but this time it was more—*she was shifting.* She tried to control it, tried to *stop* it, but she couldn't. Her wolf was in agony and needed to come out.

She snapped through the shift and lurched to Jared's side. She lay her furry head on his chest, listening for a heartbeat. In the shocked silence that followed her shifting, she could just barely hear the thumping of his heart, slow and weak. Her wolf whined for him and nuzzled into him, oblivious to what was going on around her. She didn't care—all she wanted was for Jared to be all right.

"Stop that!" That was her father's voice, but it was directed at Agent Smith, stopping him from something. "Goddammit, Grace! Get away from him!"

She blinked up at her father, seeing him through her wolf's eyes for the first time. He was large and angry and hovering over her. Somehow the look on his face—concern stirred around with anger—snapped her out of her haze. But it was the gun sticking in her face—a gun in Sanders's hand—that forced her to back away from both men on all four paws.

She focused inwardly, closing her eyes and regaining control enough to shift human.

"Put that thing away!" her father said, but not to her.

The man—Sanders or Agent Smith, her father had called him—lowered his weapon. Grace scrambled for her clothes, which had been shed when she shifted.

She was crying and shaking and had no idea what she was doing. Her brain was completely in shock, and she was acting on instinct, but she had to think of some way out of this. They needed to call an ambulance for Jared. But her father's hard looks, and the fact that Agent Smith *still* hadn't put away his gun, fuzzed out her brain even more. She could barely stand upright to get her clothes on.

Her father sighed, but anger still colored his face a blotchy red. "Why didn't you tell me, Grace?" He shook his head at her, sad and disgusted.

"Tell you?" She managed to blurt out. "I've been trying to tell you! But you refused to listen. You refused to care. And now this…" Jared's unmoving body captured her—she couldn't look away from it. "How can you *do* this? What kind of man *are* you?"

Her father gritted his teeth. "The human kind. The kind I thought *you* were. I really wish you would have told me before now—I could've spared you this indignity."

"Indignity?" She felt like she was losing her mind, standing in front of these two men in her bare feet and disheveled clothes, having just revealed her wolf. Agent Smith was eyeing her with particular care, like she had just become extremely interesting to him. She swung back to her father. "What the hell you talking about?"

"I thought…" Her father rubbed his face with both hands, and the anger morphed into a kind of weariness. "I thought I was safe with you, Grace. Usually, the shifter gene expresses much earlier. How long have you been shifting?"

She just gaped at him. "What... are you saying... you *knew?*"

"I *didn't* know," he sneered. "I merely suspected. After I caught your mother with that damn shifter, I did the math. I knew it was possible. I just hoped... *goddammit.*" He was shaking his head, but those final words were just mumbled to himself.

"You knew." The shock was washing over her anew. "You knew all along."

He dismissed her with a wave, like she was yesterday's news, then turned to Agent Smith. "I need you to get rid of this... this *thing.*" He gestured to Jared's body. "I don't want to start my campaign with unexplained bodies of bodyguards, especially in shifter form, in my office."

Agent Smith narrowed his eyes at Jared's fallen form. "This *is* rather inconvenient." He finally put away his tranq gun.

They were ignoring her completely. Her body buzzed, numb.

"If we take him into custody," Agent Smith said, "his pack will just come after him. Better to just kill him and dispose of the body."

Terror ripped through Grace's body. *"What? You can't... you... you need to call a doctor!"* Her head was pounding, and the world felt like it was tipping.

"I told you, no bodies," her father muttered to Agent Smith. "Especially ones that could be traced back here."

"I'll make sure that won't happen," Agent Smith said coolly.

Her father shook his head. "Fine." He glanced at Grace, but then spoke to Agent Smith. "What about her? You've got the serums now. Can you cure her?"

Grace stared at the two of them in horror. What was he saying?

"I can try." Agent Smith peered at her. "It might be possible. Although maybe not. And if not, what then?"

Her father waved that concern away. "We'll cross that bridge when we get there."

Agent Smith advanced toward her. "Come with me, Ms. Krepky."

She backed up. "Wha... what are you talking about?"

Her father sighed again, returning to his desk. "I wish you had told me, Grace. We could have gotten you help sooner."

"Help? What kind of help?" But a primal fear raced through her. *Cure?* That meant… God, what were they going to do to her? The specter of Jared's medical experiments rose up in her mind. The Senator wouldn't do that to his own daughter. *Would he?*

Her father gestured to Agent Smith, encouraging him to proceed. "Take her away. Give it a try. I can't have her here like this."

Her eyes went wide with horror. "Daddy—"

His eyes went hard. "I am *not* your father. Obviously." He turned his back on her.

Agent Smith made a grab for her. She shrunk away, and in desperation, shifted to her wolf form, hoping to make a run for it. She scrambled past him, but she didn't even make it to the door before three rapid pinches sunk into her back. The world blurred, and she slumped against the still-closed door.

Her vision started to fade. The last thing she saw was Jared's wolf form lying on the cool marble floor of her father's office.

Chapter Thirteen

Jared heard wailing in the distance.

He was lying on something hard and foul-smelling, and everything hurt. A moan creaked out of him before he managed to open his eyes. The wailing sound wasn't a human cry—or a wolf howl —but something mechanical. Pitched high. Pitched low. Back and forth as he slowly opened his eyes.

He tried to move, but he was weak. The room was dimly lit, afternoon light filtering in through slatted blinds. A shaky voice came from behind him, muttering words his barely-conscious brain couldn't make out. He tried to push up from the musty carpet and twist around to see who it was, but a wave of dizziness sent him back down again. The shrill voice screeched louder behind him.

He vaguely remembered that Agent Smith had showed up at the Senator's office and shot him— but Jared had no idea where he was now.

He stayed down, closer to the floor this time, and just turned his head to peer into the striped shadows. A woman was standing on a bed in the middle of the room, which was some kind of cheap motel, judging by the odor, the crappy bedspread, and the barely-patched holes in the wall.

Most of all, he noticed the gun shaking in her hand and pointing at him. "Don't move! Don't move! Oh God, he's moving!"

Jared tried to get his hands up and tell her to calm down, but all that came out was a moan and an awkward flailing. The gun went off, and white-hot pain tore through his shoulder, throwing him flat on the floor again.

The woman screamed.

"Fuck," Jared breathed out. What the hell was going on?

"Oh God! Oh God! I shot him!" The woman was hysterical.

Jared blinked, fighting off another wave of dizziness. His shoulder screamed with fresh pain, but his entire body was body weak and on fire. He swallowed hard, but stayed down, so she wouldn't shoot him again. When he thought he could speak intelligibly, he waited for a pause between her screaming and ranting.

"I'm not going to hurt you!" he called out.

Her rambling cut off suddenly. He lifted his head to peer at her. She was still on the bed, but the gun was at her side, and she was staring at the window. The mechanical wailing grew closer and louder.

When she saw him watching her, the hand with the gun popped back up. "That man said to shoot you if you woke up!" The gun wavered. She was barely dressed, mostly in fishnet. Her tight corset heaved with her panic.

She was obviously some kind of street worker roped into this situation by Agent Smith. Jared shook his head and tried to piece it together. If some poor woman claimed Jared had attacked her, and she shot him in self-defense... either he would end up dead from her gun or he would simply go to jail. Either way, Jared would be out of the way for whatever Agent Smith's plans were. And the Senator's.

Grace. God, what happened to her? There was no way she would take this sitting down. He had to find her.

The woman was still pointing the gun at him.

Jared raised a shaky hand. "I'm not going to hurt you," he repeated, more softly. "Just put the gun down. I don't know what he's paying you to do this, but trust me—it's not worth going to jail for murder." He had to stop for a moment, gasping for air. This raspy kind of weakness... it was bad news. He'd lost too much blood. He needed to get out before the police arrived, or he'd bleed out before he reached the station.

He squinted up at the woman's terrified face. "This is not your problem. Just put the gun down, and I'll walk away. None of this has to be your problem."

Her eyes were wide, but he could tell that shooting him the first time had freaked her out. She slowly lowered the gun again. Jared worked his way to his feet. The siren was insanely close—they were probably pulling into the parking lot already. He was a mess—covered in blood, naked—but at least he was human. A wolf would be shot on sight.

Jared stumbled toward the door, threw it open, and lumbered to the back of the motel. He managed to slip around the corner before the crunch of police car tires rolled up to the room where he had just been. It wouldn't take long for them to come after him, and the way he was bleeding, he'd probably leave a trail. He needed some speed, and for that, he needed his wolf. He would just have to stay out of sight.

He shifted and tore like hell down the side street behind the motel. Then he slowed his pace because he was in danger of passing out, even in magic-enhanced wolf form. He lumbered down the alley, past the back doors of a whole line of businesses, until he'd put a good two or three blocks between him and the police.

Finally, he found a door to one of the shops propped open. He shifted human, yanked on the rusted-out metal door, and stumbled inside. The back half of the store was a warehouse filled with boxes of supplies. One was marked *ice cream cones.* A screech of childish laughter trickled in from the front. Jared grabbed an apron off a hook and slung it over his neck, managing to cover some of his nakedness before he shoved open another door marked *office.*

Inside was a phone and no people. *Thank God.* He collapsed into the desk chair and dialed his brother, Jace.

"Hey, bro, how did the political machinations—"

"Jace." Jared's wheezy voice cut him off.

"*Jesus!* Jared, are you all right?"

"No."

A peal of laughter came from the front. *Shit.* The last thing those kids needed was to stumble in on a bleeding half-naked man in the back. Not to mention, they'd call the cops. From the phone in his hand came sounds of shouting and scrambling.

Jace's voice barked in his ear. "I'm grabbing Jaxson, and we're getting in the car. What's your location?"

Jared slumped in the chair, struggling to even stay upright. "Bring your med kit. I need stitching." He could hear the wheeze in his voice getting worse. The room started to spin. Or maybe it was the chair. He gripped the edge of the desk to keep everything from moving.

"Stay with me, Jared." That was Jaxson's voice. "Jace wants me to talk to you and keep you awake, so don't let your lazy ass fall asleep on me." There is a brief muffled sound, then, "Location! We need to know where you are, Jared. You're not on your cell."

"Ice cream store." His vision was beginning to blur. "Kids. Lots of kids. Birthday party maybe." His head was slowly sinking to the desk, and he couldn't seem to stop it. He just needed to rest for a little bit—then he could maybe get up and see where he was. Find an address...

"Jared! Wake up!"

But he couldn't keep his eyes open any longer. He set the phone on the table, then laid his head down. So tired. The world slowly went black.

Muffled voices woke him this time. Then rough hands jostled him. A dozen of them. They lifted him up and carried him... somewhere. By the time he opened his eyes, he was in the back of one of the pack's vans. Jace was bending over him, flashing a light in his eyes that made him squint.

"He's conscious," Jace told someone, not him. Then he lightly tapped Jared's face. "Stay with me, bro. I need to stitch you up. This might hurt a little."

Jared nodded shakily. "No scars," he wheezed. "This time."

Jace smirked. "Don't worry, I'll leave you pretty enough for Grace." Then the humor dropped off his face, and his brother dug into a kit next to Jared. A moment later, he was digging into Jared. He must've swum in and out of consciousness for a while, because the next thing he knew, he was waking up on a much softer surface.

He was back in his bed at the safehouse.

Jace and Jaxson were both in his room, along with their mother. All three of them wore faces fit for a funeral. Jared tried to struggle up to sitting, but he was crazy weak. Jace saw him first and jumped out of his chair next to the bed to push Jared back down.

"Don't be an idiot," Jace said. "I mean, more than you usually are. You lost a lot of blood. You need to rest." But he looked relieved to see Jared awake.

His mother and Jaxson gathered around the bed as well, worried looks on their faces.

"I'm good," Jared said, but he could feel the weakness in it. *Shit.* He was a mess. And Grace was still... he didn't know. "Where's Grace?"

They exchanged looks. Jace spoke first. "We don't know."

"How long have I been out?" Jared asked. It usually only took him a few hours to recover once he got stitched up.

"About ten hours," Jaxson said quietly, frowning.

Damn, Jared thought. He'd been out ten hours and still felt like shit? He must have been close to punching out. And for once… he was really glad that he didn't.

"I'll get him something to eat," his mom said, then scurried toward the door.

Jared wanted to sit up, but Jace was still looming over him. He had that *I'm an Army Shifter Medic, don't mess with me* look. He'd probably dose Jared with something to keep him down if he had to.

Jared managed to keep him back with a scowl. "I need to go after Grace."

"You're in no shape to go after anyone." Jaxson exchanged a look with Jace, who nodded. "But if you tell us what's going on, then we can do what needs to be done."

Jared sucked in a breath. Some of his strength was returning, but it was still pretty bad. "Grace was going to tell the Senator she was a shifter, but before she could, Agent Smith showed up."

Jaxson's eyebrows flew up. *"Holy shit."*

"Those would've been my exact words," Jared said with a nod, "but I was too busy trying to kill him. He shot me and dumped me at some motel, trying to get rid of me, I think, while keeping all of it away from the Senator. But all this could've blown back on Grace. I need to know if she got out of that room okay. Agent Smith tranqed me—I don't know what happened to her."

"Okay, okay," Jace said, holding his hands up to placate Jared. "We'll find out what we can about Grace."

"We don't have time to mess around." Jared struggled to sit up again, and this time he batted away his brother's hands as Jace tried to stop him. "You're not going to stop me from going after her."

Jace gave an elaborate sigh, and Jaxson just shook his head.

"Well, I'm glad to see you're just stubborn and not doing something stupid that might result in your death." Jaxson gave him a hard look.

Jace pulled out his cell phone. "I'll just check in with Garrison Allied—"

"No!" Jared said, making a swipe for the phone but missing so awkwardly it was clear he was in no shape to do anything. But he had to keep his brothers from screwing things up… worse than they already were. "Garrison Allied's already in deep shit the Senator. I was undercover, remember? He's probably already reamed them a new one. They're not going to help us." He rested his head in his hands. It was throbbing, but at least it wasn't spinning like he remembered before the surgery. "The key is Agent Smith. He's obviously still here in Seattle, and we know he's working with the Senator. There has to be some way to track him. And you should call the campaign office and ask for Grace. If she's okay, she'd be going about her normal business, and that's where she would be."

Jaxson frowned, but he didn't disagree. "All right, here's the deal: you stay here, get some rest, and Jace and I will track down these leads. If you're not resting, then we have to sit here and babysit you to make sure you heal up the rest of the way and can be worth a damn in helping us rescue her. If that's even necessary."

Jared couldn't deny the weakness that was still running through his body. He wouldn't be any good to Grace if he just collapsed while trying to rescue her. Still… it was killing him not to crawl out of the bed and go after her. With great reluctance, he gave Jaxson a small nod of agreement and leaned back against the pillows of his bed.

Jace was heading for the bedroom door, but turned back to ask, "Do you still have that facial recognition software program running?"

"Yeah. That's good thinking." It was a testament to how messed up he was that he hadn't thought of it first. "If Agent Smith's in Seattle, we should be able to line up some of those traces. And, Jace, he's using an alias—at least in his dealings with the Senator. Name is Robert Sanders. You might get some hits on that."

"I'm on it." Jace disappeared out the door. Jaxson hurried after him.

Jared sunk into the softness of the pillows. He would just take a short nap, then call his brothers back up. Or go hunt them down. If Jace had done his job sewing him up, it shouldn't take long for Jared to get back to full strength. The fact that he'd only just now woken up was a bad sign… but a little more rest should do it. His body felt like it weighed ten times normal as he let himself relax. Sleep grabbed him and threw him down a deep, dark well.

When Jared awoke this time, the sun had gone down and moonlight was already shining through his bedroom window. But when he sat up, his headache was gone and a new sense of energy flushed through his body. He tested it out by swinging his legs over the side the bed, and when they felt steady, he got up. He stretched out the aches and pains—and noticed he had several new scars—but he felt pretty good. Probably about eighty percent.

Which was plenty good enough to go after Grace.

With any luck, she would have spent the day doing campaign activities. He kind of hoped she worried about him, just a little… and that hope was a strange sensation inside his chest. Not that he really wanted her to worry. But he did. Along with the urgent desire to believe the connection between them wasn't just in his imagination.

He quickly washed up and threw on some fresh clothes, then trotted down the stairs. Even that jostling didn't hurt him. He was feeling better with each step.

A war room had been set up in the dining room just outside the kitchen. Jaxson, Jace, Piper, and even Olivia, along with Owen and a couple of the other pack members, were crowded around the table. Maps and printouts and tablets scrolling information crowded the surface.

"Sleeping beauty has arisen," Jace said with a smirk.

That must mean Jared was off the medical watch list.

"Whatever you guys are doing, I'm ready to do my part." Jared gestured to the table. "What do you have?"

"We're just working out a plan of action," Jaxson said. "So your timing for getting back in the game is pretty good. How do you feel?"

Jared frowned. He was standing, wasn't he? "I'm good. Did you find Grace?"

"Well, sort of." Jace picked up an image of an office building and held it up for Jared. "We think she's in here."

Piper tapped the image. "You're never going to guess what this is."

"Agent Smith's day job as a middle manager?" Jared was surprised he had any sense of humor at all in him. He shut that down pretty quick and chalked it up to the heady recovery.

"Supposedly it's the headquarters for an import-export logistics company," Piper said with a smirk. "It's an open secret in intelligence circles, however, that it's the local NSA office."

National Security Agency—the feds. *"Shit."* Jared humor faded quickly. "Why is Grace there?"

Jaxson gathered up several more images. "We've

been tracing Agent Smith's pings on your facial recognition software. This morning, about the time you were at the Senator's estate, we found several hits tracking him through cameras on street surveillance and local banks. Then he went off grid. The last image has him pulling into the parking lot of the NSA's secret HQ. We didn't know what it was until Piper clued us in."

"So you know Agent Smith is there, but not Grace?" Jared frowned again. "Did you check her office?"

Jaxson nodded. "The party line at the campaign headquarters is that she's home with the flu."

Jared ground his teeth. "So the Senator's got a cover story already. One that will keep her out for a while." This was getting worse and worse.

Piper nodded and gave him a knowing look. "We know Grace was in the car with Agent Smith as he pulled into the parking lot. We've got seven red light camera images just before he arrived—all with a man fitting Agent Smith's description, and a woman with long brown hair like Grace. Although she looked like she was sleeping."

Jared momentarily squeezed his eyes shut. *Smith had her.* Jared had waited too long.

"And he's still in there," Jaxson added. "We've

had surveillance on him from the moment we knew he was inside."

Piper gave Jared a concerned look, like she was reading his thoughts. "We can't just storm in there," she chastised him, then glanced at Jaxson and Jace. "We've been debating the options, and we figure the best is falsified ID. I can get you clearance through my office. I was going to go in myself, but I can hook you up. Unless you're not feeling up to it…"

"No. I'm doing this." It came out harsher than he meant.

Piper just nodded, like she expected that answer. Jared narrowed his eyes at his brothers, daring them to stop him.

Jace just held up his hands. "Hey, I was voting for waiting until you woke up. No way I wanted to answer to you for having sent my mate after yours."

His mate. Jared's throat closed up. Because inside, deep where his wolf lived, he already knew she was. If she would have him.

He cleared throat, and the sound carried in the silence that had suddenly dropped across the room. "Right. I'm going after my mate."

Chapter Fourteen

WHEN GRACE AWOKE, SLOWLY SWIMMING OUT OF
the haze the tranquilizer, she was inside a cage.

It was the kind of cage you would put a dog in
—a very large dog, but still nowhere near large
enough for a human. She was lying down, but when
she sat up, her head almost grazed the top of the
fine steel mesh. She rubbed at the blurriness in her
eyes, not quite believing she was caged like an
animal. As she blinked and focused beyond the thin
metal bars, she jerked with surprise.

Agent Smith sat outside her cage in a swivel
chair. It was an ordinary office chair—black, cush-
ioned—and he was slowly rotating it, back and
forth.

"Nice to see you awake, Ms. Krepky." His eyes glittered, a small smile tugging at his lips.

A shudder ran through her, but she didn't answer, just whipped her gaze around the room to see where she was. It looked like a lab—stainless steel countertops and cabinets and a gurney at one end. The smell of steel and antiseptic tinged sour on her tongue and competed with the sickness rising at the back of her throat. Whatever this place was, her father knew about it… and sent her here. He had turned her over to Agent Smith, casting her aside like yesterday's trash as soon as he knew she wasn't his biological daughter.

And Jared… *God,* Agent Smith shot him *three times.* Was he dead? She knew from personal experience how fast shifters could heal, but there was a limit… even a tough Marine would have a hard time surviving being shot at point-blank range. The horror of that—of losing him, of it being her fault —ripped through her, gutting her out. Her wolf howled a mournful cry.

"If you're thinking of screaming," Agent Smith said, "don't bother. We're in a basement that I long ago outfitted with the best in noise suppression. No one comes down here, and you aren't the first visitor I've had."

Fear for herself pushed through her agony about Jared and seized hold of her chest. But she wasn't going to let her father just dispose of her. Or let this Agent Smith person experiment on her. She was determined to find a way out, and for that she needed more information.

"What have you done with Jared?" She edged forward, up on her knees, and grasped onto the cage door. The construction was pretty flimsy. Maybe she could wrench the door off its hinges once Agent Smith left her alone.

His smile grew. "I'm sure he's bled out by now. Although I'm kind of hoping he caught a couple extra bullets before that happened. A little more pain for one of the River brothers would make my day."

The anger rose up in her, and she gripped the cage harder, curling her fingers around the metal and pushing against it to test its strength. "So you enjoy inflicting pain on people. Nice. Don't you ever look in the mirror, Agent Smith, and wonder what went wrong with your life?"

He smirked. "I'm not the one in the cage." Then he cocked his head to the side. "Your father was surprised to find out you were a shifter, but he should have known better, especially given your mother couldn't keep her pants on."

The thin bars of the cage bit into her hand. "You don't know anything about my mother."

His smile grew. "Your father let his wishful thinking get in the way of the truth—that anyone can be a shifter. In fact, that's the problem. They're hiding under the skin of everyone around us, waiting to seduce our women and impregnate them with their spawn. That's what you are, Grace. The unwanted bastard child of a transient shifter who fucked your mother and left her behind. Your father told me the story. Did he ever tell you?"

She banged her fist against the cage door, and it rattled the entire thing. "All I need to know about my father is that I'm here. With you."

Agent Smith wheeled his chair closer, leaning forward and putting his elbows on his knees, templing his fingers. He was getting way too much pleasure out of this. "Yes, you are, Ms. Krepky. And I cannot wait to get started with you."

The cold trickle in her stomach surged up into a gush, a tsunami of fear that washed through her body. She leaned away from him, then scuttled backward until she bumped against the wire mesh —the cage just wasn't big enough to go anywhere.

He licked his lips, and Grace's stomach lurched. "There are so many things I want to do with you, Grace, but don't worry—having sex with you is *not* one of them."

She supposed that should make her feel better, but it didn't. This Agent Smith character got off on hurting people… he might not rape her, but that didn't mean he wasn't going to hurt her. And enjoy it in the process.

Words caught in her throat, but she sucked in a breath and forced them out. "My father said he doesn't like dead bodies." She hoped that was actually true. Except it sounded like Agent Smith had already killed Jared. Which made her heart squeeze again, forcing tears to burn at the back of her eyes.

"Oh, I'm not going to kill you. But we *will* have some fun along the way."

He was trying to scare her, so she refused to let his creepy words rattle her. "Your idea of fun is one of those things that comes with a diagnosis. What do you want from me?"

"Well, for starters, I'd like you to shift." He folded his arms and leaned back in his chair. "You seem to have a little trouble controlling your wolf. But that's not anywhere near the most unique thing about you, is it, Grace?"

"What are you talking about?" She honestly didn't know.

"For one, the color of your fur. I'm intrigued by your unique lineage—I'd almost thought the white wolf was only legend. But here you are—different and conveniently in my cage. Your father doesn't know who impregnated your mother, although I suspect he plans to use the general registration program to track him down." Agent Smith lifted one eyebrow. "How does that saying go? *All politics is personal.* Certainly true in your father's case."

Grace was beginning to wonder if it was true in Agent Smith's case as well—or if he just had some deep loathing for shifters programmed into his DNA. She was still coming to grips with the idea that her biological father was a shifter… but she hadn't gotten to the point of wondering *who* that shifter might be. Or where he might've gone. He obviously didn't stick around long.

"I don't suppose you know who your true father is," Agent Smith tried.

She narrowed her eyes. "Why does it even matter?"

He rose up out of his chair and loomed over her cage. "It matters because understanding shifters is *everything.* It's the key to keeping control of our world. Your father's legislation is the culmination of the effort, not the beginning. I have been working on this for *years*—studying, analyzing, tracking down shifters, showing how pervasive they are in our society and how much of a danger they are to it." He gestured to her. "You're a prime example, Grace. You're exactly what I don't want to see happen." He wrinkled up his nose, disgusted. "Humans breeding with shifters. Polluting our DNA with your genes. Ruining our families and our bloodlines. Most shifters mate with each other, and if they simply kept to that, it would be bad enough. But you don't restrain yourselves, do you? You and your wanton sexuality, seducing the human population and creating halfling abominations like yourself. It has to be stopped."

Grace's eyes slowly went wide as she listened to his hate-filled and frankly irrational ranting. This *had* to be personal for him to feel this much loathing. "So this is all about... segregation? You want to keep humans and shifters apart?"

Agent Smith shrugged one shoulder. "That doesn't go anywhere near far enough. Your father's legislation will flush out the shifters hiding among our population. Then we can domesticate the animals, turn them into non-shifters permanently, so they can't corrupt the gene pool. This beast nature of yours has to be controlled, Grace. *Cured.*" His lip curled back as he said it.

Grace was shaking again. "I don't need to be cured!"

"You're *unnatural.* Something I'm going to fix." He gestured around the empty basement lab where she was being held prisoner. "My operations have been curtailed lately—those River brothers managed that much—but it doesn't matter. I already have the serums I need. I can cure you of your base animal tendencies, as well as use the shifter genetic serums I've developed as a weapon against our enemies. At least in that way, your kind can prove useful." He crouched down next to her cage door. "Now, Grace, how about you shift for me? I need a sample of that blood of yours in shifter form with that unique fur color."

Grace lifted her chin in defiance. "I'm not cooperating with you."

A small smirk grew on his face. "I was hoping you might say that. I'd be happy to have a witch force you to shift, but bringing witches into the building is a little… *inconvenient.* But there are other ways to accomplish the same goal, especially for a young woman like yourself who's particularly inexperienced at controlling her wolf."

The gleam in his eye made her physically ill. She didn't want to cooperate, but she knew she couldn't control her wolf. She'd already lost it once, in her father's office, revealing herself. She was sure she would lose whatever game Agent Smith wanted to play.

"That won't be necessary." Grace closed her eyes and forced herself to shift. She wasn't sure what would happen next, but when she opened her eyes as a wolf, Agent Smith already had a gun out. A familiar pinch pierced her fur coat. Darkness swam around her, and she lost control of her limbs, slumping to the floor.

The last thing she heard was, "Thank you for your cooperation, Grace."

Then the darkness closed in.

This time, when Grace started to wake up, she kept her eyes closed.

She was lying on something hard and flat and cold. There were bindings holding her down, across her ankles and hands and chest. The same smell of steel and antiseptic pervaded her nose. Even before she opened her eyes, she knew where she was—the gurney. A sickening drop in her stomach accompanied that realization.

She opened her eyes—Agent Smith sat next to her in that same spinning office chair. Only this time he looked pissed. A glance down at her body, showed she was back to human. She had no recollection of shifting—it must've happened while she was out.

Agent Smith loomed closer with his angry face. "I need you to shift again, Grace."

She scowled at him. "What? Did you spill all the blood you took the first time?"

He spoke through gritted teeth. "Your shifting ability is apparently unstable even when you're unconscious. You had the annoying tendency of shifting back and forth. Then you shifted human and stayed that way." He glared at her like he thought she had foiled him on purpose.

"I was *unconscious.* It's not like I could control it." She gave him a look like he was a nutjob. Which he obviously was.

She needed to focus on getting out of this mess, but her thoughts kept drifting to Jared. The idea of him being dead just surged tears to her eyes and threatened to break her heart into pieces. He was just starting to live again… her wolf broke out into a pitiful cry. Grace had to shove her mind away from those thoughts. She could mourn Jared properly once she was free. Or find him… she still held out the faintest of hopes that he had survived. Shifters were tough, and that man was the toughest she had ever seen. *Marine tough.* But she had to acknowledge the reality—she was on her own here. No one was coming to rescue her.

Agent Smith rose up from his chair and loomed over the gurney. "Are you going to shift for me again, Grace? Or do I need to persuade you?"

The gush of fear was back, but her rising anger fought against it. "You had your chance. I'm not playing your games anymore!"

He snarled and reached over to somewhere she couldn't see… then came back with something that glinted silver in his hand. She twisted to take a look —the scalpel caught the overhead lights in its stainless steel polish.

"Wait…" she said, suddenly finding it hard to breathe. "What are you doing?"

He didn't answer, just grabbed hold of her hand, which was bound by a leather cuff, flipped it over to expose the back, and quickly whipped the scalpel across it. A sharp pain jumped from her hand and raced up her arm.

She couldn't help crying out, more from the shock than the pain. She lifted her head and stared with horror at the blossoming red line. Agent Smith wiped the blood from the scalpel on a small cloth and dropped it next to her.

"Too bad your human blood doesn't have quite the same properties as your shifter blood. But I'm quite willing to extract as much of it as necessary to get you to shift."

The stinging pain of the slice quickly faded. But when she didn't shift immediately, Agent Smith took another swipe across her hand, making her cry out again.

"You sick fuck!" The pain faded quickly again —she'd always healed super fast from her scrapes and sprains as a child. She knew it was a shifter trait, so she had kept it hidden from her father. But even at a young age, she knew it was unusual.

Agent Smith had this twisted look on his face. "Don't talk dirty to me, Ms. Krepky." He snorted at his own joke, but it sent even more chills through her. He retrieved the cloth to wipe the scalpel again and swiped roughly at her hand to clear away the blood.

Then he stared at the back of her hand.

Grace knew the cuts would be gone by now, probably leaving behind faint white lines like they usually did.

A frown slowly morphed his face from the sick, twisted look of enjoyment to one so intense it freaked her out even more. Then he slammed her hand down flat to the gurney and dove into it with the scalpel.

The pain was *insane*... like he was cutting off her hand! A scream ripped her throat.

He pulled back, holding the bloody scalpel aloft. Shaking with horror, she lifted her head to look— massive amounts of blood gushed up to obscure most of her hand, but the bone and fleshy stubs of muscle were sticking out. Her stomach lurched at the sight. But as she watched, the muscles writhed like snakes, stitching themselves back together. The rest was lost under a coating of blood.

Agent Smith stared open-mouthed at her hand. Then he grabbed the cloth again and roughly scrubbed away the blood. It hurt a little because she was still healing, but by the time he wiped the blood away, she could tell without looking that it was fixed.

The horror on his face would've been gratifying,

except he still held the bloody scalpel aloft, and that sent lightning strikes of terror through her body.

"Extraordinary," he whispered, still staring at her now-healed hand. He slowly dragged his gaze up to hers. "You heal very quickly, Ms. Krepky."

A sickening dread ran through her with those words. She lifted her trembling chin to him. "It's just what shifters do."

His eyes widened a little. "You've been isolated. Kept away from other shifters. What would you know about what shifters can do... and not." He almost was talking to himself, not to her.

She scowled, but at least he was putting the scalpel down. Then he seemed to think better of that and snatched it back up again, holding it up to her face.

She shrunk away, crying out an inarticulate sound of fear. *"Stop!"*

He got in her face, close enough to smell his foul breath. "Shift!" he demanded, his lips twitching with anger and a bizarre kind of insanity.

"Okay, I will, I swear!" She squeezed her eyes shut, turning away from him and focusing on calling her wolf. A moment later, she had shifted, but she was still trapped on the gurney with bindings at her feet and hands that seemed to shrink to her form. A wide leather strap across her chest also held her down.

She looked back to Agent Smith, to make sure he had put away the scalpel. He had taken several steps back, looking at her with wide eyes again, this time in shock. "You shifted," he whispered to himself.

Wasn't that what he wanted? *Fuck*, this guy was straight-up crazy.

He pointed the scalpel at her but kept his distance. "Shift back to human!" he ordered.

She did, struggling to worm her way back into her clothes during the shift. Her skirt managed to stay in place during the change, but her blouse was half off her shoulder, and her bra was down around her waist. She was in danger of being exposed, but that was the least of her problems.

Agent Smith stalked over with the scalpel, brandishing it in front of her face again. "I gave you the suppressor! How are you still able to shift?" Spittle was forming at the edges of his mouth. "What's so special about you, Grace? What is this... this... unnatural ability to heal? Is it related to your rare pigment? Have you always had this ability?"

At least she could answer that last one. "Yes, as long as I can remember. I've always healed pretty much instantly." She hoped that would keep the scalpel from coming closer.

But his eyes continued to hold a kind of horror. "This isn't something to cure," he said, talking to himself again. "This is way too valuable." He snapped his fingers, excited about some thought inside his crazy head. "The serums... the side effects... this would eliminate them." He looked back to her with wild eyes. "Our attempts to create super soldiers have been hapless at best. The subjects are hard-pressed to withstand the change. But if they had this ability—this enhanced healing ability of yours—then there is literally nothing we couldn't do."

Her mouth dropped open. Super soldiers? *What the hell?*

The crazy in his eyes just simmered up to high. "How far does this super healing of yours go?"

"I... I don't know..." She was having a hard time breathing.

"Maybe we need to find out."

He came at her with the scalpel again.

She screamed until she was hoarse... and prayed someone would hear.

Chapter Fifteen

JARED CRUISED INTO THE NONDESCRIPT OFFICE building as if he actually belonged there.

Piper had worked up an ID for him, complete with his photo and all the right security protocols, but it was nine o'clock at night and pretty suspicious for him to be straggling into work.

Or maybe not, given this was an NSA building. They must have all kinds of unconventional activities. But security also had to be tight. His cover story of visiting from another division with some kind of high clearance waiver to get inside without an escort would hopefully hold up. It wasn't far from the truth, given Piper had pulled in all her favors to make this happen. Jared didn't know what the NSA was up to or how Agent Smith could be conducting secret experiments on shifters without them knowing, but everything was compartmentalized in intelligence. The right hand didn't know what the left hand was doing, most of the time, by design. So it was possible Agent Smith had gone off book, and his activities weren't officially sanctioned, at least by the NSA.

Clearly the Senator approved.

A guard with a badge that read "Johnson" gave Jared a dark-eyed stare as he passed the ID through the scanner. Jared hadn't brought a weapon of any kind—Piper had warned him about the weapons scanner. Even if he was permitted to carry, they might check the registration. Which would not bode well for actually getting past the checkpoint.

"Good evening," Jared said, trying to appear cool yet friendly. Definitely not someone sneaking in with falsified ID.

Johnson just gave him a nod and raised a hand to keep him from cruising through the weapons arch. The guard checked Jared's ID on the computer at his station. Apparently, the clearance via scan wasn't sufficient.

It took an agonizing ten seconds, but Johnson finally waved him through the arch. Thankfully, Jared's hidden mic and earbud didn't set it off.

Then again, they *were* mainly plastic, designed for minimum detectability, and he currently had them switched off. He was going into this with his shifter abilities and an urgent need to rescue Grace, but not much else.

Once he was down the hall and around the corner, striding past offices that appeared locked, he activated his earbud and the microphone sewn into the collar of his white dress shirt.

"All right, I'm in," he whispered. Jace was on the other end to guide him. Taylor, their computer whiz within the pack, had tricked out Jared's phone to help with some of the security measures he might encounter, but mostly the pack was on standby outside, in case Jared got into trouble he couldn't get out of—then they would come and get him and Grace the hell out of there by force.

Which was no one's preferred option.

If they *all* got caught, Olivia had documentation ready to go public—hopefully, that would pull them out of whatever government tangle they found themselves in. It was a great plan, except he had no idea where Grace actually was inside the building.

"Okay," Jace said over the tiny earbud stuck way inside Jared's ear. "I need you to get your phone next to one of the security scanners by a door. Hopefully, Taylor's hack will let you access the entry and exit log, so we can track down Agent Smith. Or Sanders. If he's calling himself something else, it might be a little more tricky."

"Copy that." Jared shuffled quietly down the hall. The whole place seemed to have emptied out, at least on this level. He fished his phone out of his pocket and held it up to one of the scanners near the end of the hall. "All right, phone in place."

His phone made a few pinging sounds, and the face of it popped up an app that was remotely activated by Taylor and running through some kind of protocol.

Jared heard a scuffle of shoes down the hall, and he leaned against the doorway, blocking what he was doing with his body. Whoever it was disappeared down another turn.

"Any chance of moving this along faster?" he asked in a whisper.

"Standby." That was Jace again. It took another ten seconds or so, but his brother finally said, "All right, Taylor says she's in the basement. Apparently, Agent Smith's been down there for most of the day."

Most of the day. *Shit.* His stomach bunched into

a hard knot, and he had to not think about Grace being in Agent Smith's grasp. His worst fears were biting at the edges of his mind—had been ever since he found out Agent Smith had her—but Jared was here, now, to get her. He had to focus on that, or his nightmares would keep him from doing what he needed to do.

Jared scanned his way into the elevator and then used his keycard to access the buttons for the basement. "There are three levels of basement here, guys," he said into the mic.

"Sanders scanned into Room 312," Jace responded. "I'm guessing third level down."

Made sense. Jared punched the number, and the elevator swooped down. When the doors opened, he stepped out but froze almost immediately. There was a distant keening that prickled the hairs on the back of his neck. It was way too high-pitched, far too much like he imagined Grace would sound if she were screaming.

He took off in the direction of the sound. "Did you hear that?" he whispered as he ran, trying to keep his footsteps light so as not to give any warning.

"Not picking up anything but your heavy breathing," Jace said.

Jared scanned the door numbers and finally found Room 312. The sound had stopped, and he hesitated at the door. Surprise was about the only thing he had going for him. He held the key card in one hand and braced his other hand on the doorknob.

"I'm going in," he whispered. Just before he scanned the key card, another scream let loose—it was definitely inside the room. His heart lurched. He shoved open the door as soon as it clicked the clearance and barreled into the room as fast as he could, but then he stumbled to a stop—Agent Smith hovered over a gurney with someone strapped to it. That someone was covered in blood, but even from across the room, Jared could see the long tumble of brown hair...

Grace.

Jared roared and shifted as he leaped across the room to reach them. Agent Smith was buried in his godforsaken act of torture, and Jared almost reached him before he could react. At the last second, the man pulled a gun from his blood-flecked G-man jacket—it went off just as Jared arrived in a blinding fury of fur and teeth and claws. A screaming pain ripped through Jared's shoulder, but his momentum barreled him into

Agent Smith and took him down. Jared lunged for his throat, just barely clamping his jaws around it when the gun went off again, this time punching Jared in the gut and loosening his hold. That fucking gun! He shifted back to human and made a grab for it. They were grappling close-quarters now. Smith was tall, but weak, at least compared to Jared's shifter strength, even with two bullets in him. He quickly wrestled the gun away, shoved it into Agent Smith's side, and pulled the trigger.

He felt the body convulse against him as the bullet ripped through. The shocked look on Agent Smith's face made it clear the bullet had done its job. Jared had seen that face many times before, usually plowed into the dirt, twisted and crumpled from his distant shot. Sometimes they wore a splatter of blood, like Agent Smith did. Sometimes it just pooled around their bodies, an inching red stain on the earth.

Jared shuddered as a warm, wet liquid slid past his knee—his naked, post-shift body was still clinging to Agent Smith's. Jared shoved away, climbing up from the floor and shakily pointing the gun at Agent Smith's head. But the man's look of shock was fixed. Jared didn't need to pull the trigger.

Smith was dead.

That didn't stop Jared from wanting to pump five more bullets into him. At the same time, he was frozen in place, hand shaking and heart racing.

A static of shouts sounded in his ear. Numbly, he dug the earbud out and dropped it to the ground to make it shut up. But the voices kept coming. Nearby. Someone was calling his name. A strangled cry of frustration finally snapped him out of his haze.

"Jared!" It was Grace, still strapped to the gurney and covered with blood. *Oh God*, the blood. Everywhere.

He dropped the gun, staggered to her side, and tried to force his shaking hands to work the straps. *"Grace, Grace…"* His damn hands were useless, bumbling. His vision blurred as her blood-soaked form lay before him. "Oh God, Grace, he hurt you." His voice was a sob. His mind was shutting down. He couldn't get the straps off. With a growl that rumbled through his entire body, he shifted one handful of claws and ripped the bindings free.

She lurched up from the gurney and wrapped her arms around his neck. The hot, slick feel of her blood sliding across his body made him nearly double over in pain. Jared should never have asked her to do this thing, this terrible, stupid thing of revealing what she was. This was all his fault. *His fault.*

His arms were shaking as they held her.

"I'm okay," she whispered against his cheek. "I promise, I'm okay."

She was hugging him and telling him everything was fine, but the world was closing down around him. Her shredded, blood-soaked clothes pressed against his naked body. Everything inside him clenched and twisted. He was turning inside out with the pain of it.

"Grace, I have to get you… Jace is outside… he can stitch you up." *God, what had he done?* Tears threatened to overwhelm him.

"Jared, look at me!" she ordered as she stepped back from him and held him at arm's length. *"I am fine!"*

She was absolutely covered everywhere in blood, and yet… somehow she was still standing. He didn't understand it.

She must be in shock.

He gently took her shoulders in his hands. They were shaking less now. "You're *not* fine, sweet Grace. Honey, he's hurt you. We need to get you some help."

ALISA WOODS

His legs were weak, probably from the gunshot wounds in his shoulder and through his side, or he'd be scooping her up in his arms right now.

She gave him a crazy half smile that blew his mind, then stepped back out of his reach to the cabinet. He watched in a daze as she grabbed a towel and started wiping herself down. Slowly the blood came off… and what was left behind astounded him. Her beautiful, creamy flesh was crisscrossed with thin white lines, but the blood… the blood all wiped away.

And there were no gaping wounds left behind.

He stumbled over to her, finally in command of his senses again, and grabbed hold of her shoulders, scanning her up and down.

She put her delicate hands on his cheeks and brought his gaze back up to hers. "I won't say it didn't hurt." Her lips trembled in a way that made him want to kill Agent Smith all over again. "But I'm all right now. I think…" She stood a little straighter. "I *know* I'm different than other shifters. I heal faster. In fact, so much so that I blew Agent Smith's mind. He decided to test the limits of how fast I could heal. Lots of times."

A lump surged up in his throat. "Oh God, Grace, I'm so sorry."

"Sorry? You're rescuing me, right? That's not something to be sorry about." She looked a little concerned now.

A small laugh bubbled up, a crazy one, so he kept it inside. "Yes, I'm rescuing you." He looked her up and down again, disbelieving, but it seemed just as she said. She had scars—so many scars, *God* —but no open wounds. Bloody clothes but no bleeding cuts. "Are you really okay? Please tell me you're okay."

She smiled. "I am now." She looked to Agent Smith's body on the floor behind him. "Please tell me he's really dead."

Jared dropped his hands from her shoulders and clenched them tight at his sides. "I want to kill him again. About ten more times for what he did to you."

Grace narrowed her eyes at the body. "I would have done it myself if you hadn't." She looked back at him, her gaze roaming over his naked, blood-covered body. Some of the blood was hers, some Agent Smith's, but some was definitely leaking out of him. "He shot you, didn't he? I heard the gun go off, but I couldn't see—"

"I'm fine, Grace." And he was, even though the pain was throbbing through his mental haze and

227

making him dizzy. But there must not be anything major hit—he wasn't crashing like he had when Agent Smith shot him the *first* three times.

She frowned. "We need to get you out of here. *Soon.* But first…" She gestured around the lab. "The serums are here. All his research is here. We have to destroy everything before we leave."

His head was buzzing with relief, but she was right—they had to think through what to do next. Agent Smith was dead. More than one shot had been fired; Jared couldn't even remember how many at this point.

"Someone will be here any second," he said. "They will have heard the gunfire."

Grace shook her head. "Maybe not. I've been screaming… well, for a long time. But this place is soundproofed. I think he brought a lot of people here."

That wrenching feeling wanted to turn him inside out again. Smith had *tortured* her. *Fuck.* He pulled her into his arms again, holding her tight. "Grace, I'm dying inside that you suffered through all this. All because of me." He was choking up again as he held her.

She pulled back and peered into his eyes. "Jared River, the only thing that got me through was the hope that I would live to find *you*. And here you are, rescuing me! You're literally the answer to all my prayers." Her eyes were shining, and her words crashed into him and stirred things around. Just like they always did.

He allowed himself a small smile. "I could say the same thing about you."

Her beautiful eyes glittered with something like hope, and it made his heart soar.

She smiled up at him. "We *definitely* need to discuss this further. Later. But right now…"

"No, you're right." He sucked in a breath—she really was all right. And they needed to focus on getting out. "Show me what we need to destroy. Then we're getting the hell out of here."

Jared scrambled to get his clothes back on, his two gunshot wounds making a mess of everything. He fumbled to make sure the microphone was still sewn into his collar, but he couldn't find the earbud.

They had to be panicking outside, so he just spoke into the mic. "I've found Grace. Agent Smith is dead. We're destroying his research. Lost audio. Will be leaving the building when we're done." Turning to Grace he said, "My brothers and the pack are waiting for us outside. They're probably losing their minds." Jared hoped they could hear that, and it would calm down whatever chaos was going on in the van.

He and Grace quickly searched the cabinets, finding hundreds of refrigerated vials. They poured out what they could into the sink and smashed the rest. But the most important research data was almost certain to be stored electronically on the computers scattered around the lab.

"Were going to have a hard time destroying all this," Jared said. There were three laptops and two desktop computers.

"That's okay," Grace said. "We're taking it with us." She snagged the laptops and handed them to Jared, then went at the desktops until she had the covers off and could dig inside. She quickly pulled out two hard drives, straggling wires behind.

Jared nodded, impressed. "Our tech guy can erase all this stuff once we're out."

"No," Grace said, firmly. "We need to preserve it. I'm going public with all this. Not the data itself, but the evidence of it. We need to show people what was going on here, Jared." She strode toward the door of the lab like she was ready to burst out into the world *right now* with all of it.

He understood the burning need to do that…

but it shot a gut-twisting worry through him. He didn't want her to get hurt. *Again.*

He caught up with her at the door. "Are you sure? Grace, your father will find a way to—"

"*My father…*" Grace hissed. "My father is the source of all of this. He sent his own daughter here to be a lab rat, tortured by a crazed anti-shifter agent of the federal government. If you don't think I'm going to let the world know about *that,* Jared River, then you don't know me as well as you think." The fire in her voice, the passion of it, her determination to right all of these wrongs—if he hadn't already fallen in love with her, he could point to this moment and say, *this is it.* This was the moment when he knew Grace Krepky was everything he wanted in a mate.

He smiled a little. "I should've known."

She frowned, and that moment of confusion held a touch of innocence again. The fiery girl ready to take on the world was replaced by the pure, good-hearted girl he had seen through his scope, the very first time, when he had decided not to kill her father—she was all those things. And goddammit, he was so in love with her.

"You should've known what?" she asked.

"That there really was a tiger underneath that

kitten exterior of yours." He smiled broadly and hoped like hell she would say *yes* when he asked. Because he was definitely asking. Not now, but soon.

She grinned. "You haven't seen anything yet, Jared River. And I know *exactly* what we need to do next."

He had no doubt.

Chapter Sixteen

JARED RIVER WAS A DAMN LIAR—HE HAD *TWO* gunshot wounds that his brother, Jace, had to sew up. That was not Grace's idea of "fine."

Regardless, once he was stitched up, he seemed to heal fast enough that she didn't need to worry about him. Too much. Her clothes were a wreck, Jared looked exhausted, and his brothers, along with the rest of the pack who had come to rescue her, all seemed completely on edge. The tension in the van was crazy high. But she knew they had no time to waste—they needed to head straight to the Senator's campaign office downtown.

"Are you sure this is a good idea?" Jared asked for the fourth time, eyeing her. She really looked a fright—with her white blouse bright with blood, and a black skirt that hid it a little better—but that was the point.

Grace could tell Jared was just voicing the other's thoughts, the ones rumbling through all the hulking, good-looking shifter men who packed the van. *Damn.* They were all extremely hot. How did female shifters get anything done with this much drool-worthy, man flesh around all the time? Even so, Jared was the largest and hottest among them. And her wolf only had eyes for him—she'd already given him her virginity, along with her heart. Now that he had saved her life, she owed even that to him. But the thing she was about to do… well, it was a bit crazy.

She hoped he would understand.

Grace gave him a nod she hoped was reassuring. "Yes, I am sure this is a good idea," she said, not just to him, but to all of them. "You want to stop the Senator, right?" She waited for the nods to grudgingly come out. "Well, I know how to do that. What's on these hard drives is all the evidence you need, but I'm uniquely suited to deliver the missile straight to the target." She held Jared's gaze. The rest of them, with all their eyes on her, faded into the background. "This isn't just for me—this for every shifter who was captured, or went under the blade, or was injected with experimental medicines. This is something I can do for all of them."

Jared just nodded. She wasn't sure if he was agreeing, or just didn't want to argue anymore, but the tension in the van dropped a couple levels. Lots of looks were exchanged, but no words during the rest of the trip back to her father's campaign office.

She insisted that only Jared accompany her. He insisted that the rest of them stay on standby outside the high-rise building. She didn't object—in fact, it was comforting to know she wasn't on her own with this. Not anymore. And looking at Jared, she hoped never again.

It was late—past ten o'clock—but she knew Kylie and Nolan and her father would still be in the office, preparing for the next day's campaign activities. They were still in ramp-up mode to the launch in a few days—everyone would be pulling late nights, under normal conditions.

Things were about to get very *not* normal.

She shoved open the door to the office and strode in. Her father, Nolan, and Kylie were all gathered in the center of the office, in the bullpen. They were huddled over Kylie's desk, examining a map of the districts, no doubt planning out a strategy to hit every precinct during the official launch—which speeches Nolan would write, which messages Kylie would tailor for the residents of each district. Her father was always intimately involved, but Grace had to wonder what he told them about his campaign manager suddenly going missing. They certainly seemed to be carrying on like nothing was wrong.

She walked up to them, Jared at her back, and stood a dozen feet away, hands on her hips, blood-stained shirt making her look like something out of a nightmare.

Kylie was the first to look up. She shrieked, and her hands flew to her face, covering her horror. Nolan and her father were next. Her father's face turned three shades more pale, and Nolan's mouth dropped open.

Nolan was the first to recover, his face flushing red as he tore around Kylie's desk. "*My God*, Grace, what happened to you?" Then he threw a glare at Jared behind her. "What the hell kind of bodyguard are you?"

"Nolan, I'm fine," Grace said, putting a hand on his shoulder, then gently shoving him back. "Jared saved my life. He's also my boyfriend." Although *boyfriend* seemed like a pretty inadequate term for their situation. He was her lover—once—

and soon to be mate. At least, she hoped. She threw a bashful look to Jared, hoping he didn't mind, but he was watching her father carefully, like he expected the Senator to pull a gun at any moment.

Which, if she was honest, was a possibility.

Nolan had a dazed look on his face. Kylie had recovered and hurried up to them. *"Jesus Christ,* Grace, why are you covered in blood?"

Grace looked away from her best friend's pained expression and stared hard at her father, who had backed away two steps, looking like he wanted to run. *Coward.* "I was tortured at the hands of a man working for the government with the blessing of my father," she declared, throwing the words at her father like knives.

He had the decency to flinch under the assault. But he didn't say anything.

"What the hell are you talking about?" Nolan was looking back and forth rapidly between her and her father.

Grace turned to face Nolan and Kylie. "My father already knows this, but it's time you did. I've been keeping a secret from you for a long time." She took a breath. "I'm a shifter."

If the shock of her in a blood-soaked shirt sent a tremor through the office, being a shifter was a

10.0 on the Richter scale. Kylie's face was blank with surprise—she stood motionless, staring at Grace with an almost comical expression on her face. Nolan looked slightly disgusted at first, but that was quickly chased away by a dawning understanding.

His gaze flitted back to her father. "Your father *knew?*" She could hear the trace of bitterness, and she couldn't blame him—after all, she had kept the secret from him even though they had supposedly dated. Nearly had sex. Had worked together intimately for years.

"He only found out today," Grace said, returning her steady drilling glare to her father. "And once he knew I wasn't his biological daughter, he packed me off into a secret program. One he had authorized to torment shifters, perform medical experiments on them, and develop serums for a shifter-based super soldier."

"*Holy fuck*—" Nolan whispered.

"Those are damn lies!" her father said, finally coming to life. "I don't know what you thought you saw—"

Grace thrust her hands into the air, one hard drive in each, ribbon wires dangling down her arms. "It's not just what I saw, *Daddy.*" The venom from hours of torture leaked into her voice. "It's not just the blade that *cut me,* time and again. Or the cage I was stuffed in. I have all the evidence I need, right here—the reams of digital data that will make your secret program not so secret anymore." Her chest was heaving. Jared's warm hand landed at the small of her back, and that affirming touch bolstered her. She kept her glare trained on her father across the room.

The Senator scowled at the hard drives in her hands. "I don't know what the hell those are—"

"Agent Smith is dead." Grace let those words hang in the air.

Her father's face opened with shock. He looked to Jared, then back to her, and Grace could see a light sheen of sweat break out on his forehead. He shuffled to the side like he was going to make a run for it.

"I don't think so." Jared stepped to block her father's path to the front door.

The Senator held back, frozen in some kind of indecision in the middle of the office.

"Who the hell is Agent Smith?" Nolan asked, his voice pitched up and panicky.

"He's the man who did this to me." Grace let her hands drop and rotated her arms so the myriad of white lines that crisscrossed them were obvious to Kylie and Nolan.

Both blinked in horror.

Nolan edged forward and took one of her hands, gently, staring at her arm. He looked up. "Oh my God, Grace. Are you all right?" His voice was soft. She could feel the sudden weight of his concern—the concern of a friend, not a jealous lover.

"I'm fine, thanks to Jared," she said with a small smile. "He saved my life. But that's not what's important now. What's important is doing the right thing." She held Nolan's gaze.

He frowned a little. "I'm not sure what you mean." But it was gentle—he wanted her to explain.

She straightened. "I will tell you exactly what I mean." She glared at her father again. "I'm going to tell the world I'm a shifter. In fact, along with that news, I'll also announce that I'm running for Congress."

Nolan just blinked at her, surprise freezing his face for the third time. Kylie covered her mouth because it was gaping wide. Her father's panicked look settled into one of fury.

"The hell you are," her father said.

"Oh, yes, I am." Grace let her anger have free rein. "And you, Senator Krepky, have a choice—either announce that you're not running for re-election and that you support my campaign, or I'll release all the information on these hard drives that explicitly connects you to the program to genetically engineer a super-soldier shifter."

"You wouldn't… you can't…" Her father was sputtering.

"Oh, I can, and I definitely will." Grace's jaw hurt when she clenched it—she'd been biting down all day, trying to survive Agent Smith's sadism and fascination with her ability to instantly heal. It made her woozy to think about, so she shoved it aside and let her righteous anger rise up. "In fact, the dirty laundry is coming out no matter what. The people deserve to know how shifters have been mistreated. How their human rights have been violated. And they deserve to have one of their own on the floor of the House to make sure something like this never happens again."

"I will not support this!" her father shouted, but his voice was screeched with panic.

"Very well," Grace said, calmly. "Then I'll show the world the scars your henchmen gave me. They can make their own judgment about a man who sent his own daughter into such a program. And all your little, bigoted friends can try to figure out where my shifter genes actually came from… and what kind of man you actually are."

Her father paled and leaned against Kylie's desk. His eyes still had that calculating look, but she could tell—he knew he was in a box with no way out.

"You're leaving me no choice at all." He looked lost, and for a brief moment, she felt bad for him. The Senate was all he knew, all he had ever wanted, and she was destroying that power dream for him. But then she reminded herself—he destroyed it the moment he sent her off with Agent Smith.

"This is your bed, Senator," she said, coolly. "I didn't make it, but I'm going make you lie in it." It felt hard—brutal almost; he *was* her father after all —but it needed to be said.

The resignation finally came across his face. He straightened up from the desk, stiffly, holding his chin up. But she knew it was just bravado. She could allow him an exit.

"I'll make the announcement tomorrow," he said.

"So will I," Grace replied.

He gave her a short nod, then strode toward the

door. He paused when he reached her and Jared, and for a moment, Grace thought Jared might just kick the crap out of him right then and there—but he held back. There was fury on Jared's face, but also a strange sort of satisfaction, as if things were working out just the way he had hoped.

Her father only spared Jared a glance, but he gave her a look full of loathing. "You will not be welcome at the estate." And with that, he strode out of the office.

If that was all he could threaten her with—that she couldn't return to her childhood bedroom—she figured that was as close as she would get to a complete and utter concession.

She heaved a sigh of relief once the door was closed behind him.

"Holy shit, Grace," Kylie said, breathless. "All this time…" She looked at Jared anew, running her eyes over him in appreciation and a kind of awe.

"I would say *holy shit* is about the least of it." Nolan's eyes were shining as he looked at her. Once he had her attention, he said, "I need to get back to work." But he didn't make a move to go anywhere.

Grace frowned. "I know you and Kylie both… well, you work for the Senator and—"

"I have a speech to write," Nolan cut her off.

243

"You're doing this tomorrow, right? And our themes are the human rights violations of shifters and cleaning up corrupt government? I can work with that."

A grin swept across her face. "Nolan..." But then she was too choked up for words. She lurched forward and threw her arms around him.

He hugged her back hard. "You sure you're okay?" he whispered into her hair.

She nodded, then released him. "I promise."

He glanced at Jared, but for once, it wasn't filled with rivalry. "He's a shifter, isn't he?"

"Yes," Grace said with a small smile for Jared. "And he's my mate."

Jared's eyes sparkled in return, but he stayed silent. He had watched the whole thing play out, quietly backing her up with his presence and his strength.

Grace looked back to Nolan. He frowned a little, but he didn't look surprised. "I can work with that, too."

She hugged him again, then Kylie shoved him aside to get her turn at hugging.

"Holy shit, girl, you do *not* mess around." Kylie grinned when she let Grace loose. "I totally would vote for you without the hot shifter man as your mate, but girlfriend, that's going to lock it down, you know what I'm saying?"

That forced a laugh out of her. Grace thought all her tears had been wrenched out, but it turned out there were a few more left inside her.

"Our country is at its best when it's practicing tolerance and respect for all people." Grace's voice boomed out over the crowd of reporters Kylie had assembled. She and Nolan stood to one side of the stage, next to Jared, who was scanning the crowd, ever vigilant for any kind of threat. He hadn't tried to talk her out of this, but he'd thrown every resource that Riverwise had into protecting her during her "coming out" speech. Dozens of hunky shifter men were sprinkled among the crowd and lined the doors to the hall.

"You don't have to be a shifter to recognize that the kind of abuses I've revealed, occurring right under our noses here in Seattle, are intolerable. We can't continue to call ourselves a civilized country if this is what we've become. If this is what we allow to happen. But I don't believe this is what we are. I believe we're a country that can find a way to accept others, no matter how different, rather than fear them. Shifters are our neighbors, our friends, our *family.* They are serving in our military, building businesses and homes and communities. They are, in a word, *us.*" She paused, letting the word stretch. The lights were hot on her face, making her squint at the crowd. They were holding their breaths, waiting for her. "It's time for a shifter to hold office. To lead us into an era where shifters no longer have to hide in the shadows or fear for their lives or hold themselves separate from society. We need shifter representation in the House precisely to keep these kinds of abuses from happening. Because that's not the kind of country we want to be. We are *better* than that."

She pulled in a breath. "Thank you for your time."

Grace stepped back from the podium. Cameras flashed. The reporters shouted questions. But Kylie had insisted that she leave all of that for later. More interviews. More speeches. This was just the beginning, and Kylie and Nolan had thrown themselves into creating a campaign for her out of thin air.

Kylie hurried forward to take the mic. "Ms. Krepky is not taking questions at this time, but there will be plenty of opportunity in the days ahead." Her best friend kept talking, placating the crowd, thanking them for their time, but Grace's head was buzzing as she stepped back to Jared's side. Nolan gave her a wide smile—she must have done okay in the delivery—then slipped away to leave her alone with the gorgeous shifter man she hoped would be her mate. Someday. Maybe soon? The long hours of the campaign loomed ahead, but the hardest part was already over.

Jared slipped his hand into hers and pulled her past the curtain, off stage. Then he tugged her into his arms and kissed the top of her head.

"You did it," he said softly, beaming down at her with pride in his eyes.

"But what did I do?" she asked, biting her lip. She had taken this insane step of revealing herself to the world. And she was making herself the spokesperson of her fellow shifters. It was risky and outrageous. And necessary. But she had no idea what Jared truly thought of all of it.

"You did the right thing. And the brave thing." He sucked in a breath, briefly squeezing his eyes closed with some kind pain, then opening them again to peer at her. "And you stopped me from killing a man."

She scrunched up her face. "Don't tell me Agent Smith is really alive!"

The pain on his face relaxed a little. "No. He's still very dead. And Piper tells me the NSA isn't eager to have his death splashed all over the news, so they've already concluded their brief investigation with the help of the FBI and decided that it was self-defense."

"So you're cleared? No charges?" It had been hanging over her heart since the night before.

"No charges." His lips pressed tight.

"Oh, thank God." She slipped her arms around his waist and rested her head on his chest. They hadn't had any time alone, not since returning to his family's safehouse the night before, crashing, then preparing for today's press conference. It felt amazingly good just to hold him.

But his arms were loose around her.

She pulled back and peered up at him. "What's wrong?"

Several tormented emotions crossed his face as he struggled for words.

She frowned. "Jared, what is it?"

He grimaced, then said, "That night… that first night. Remember how I said I was watching you?"

She cocked one eyebrow. "Pretty stalkerish, but

yeah… you were spying on my father to…" Her voice trailed off. *You stopped me from killing a man.* She blinked at him. "You were there to kill my father." She dropped her hold on him and stepped back.

He winced, eyes pinched and heavy. "Yes."

"But you didn't." Her mind was whirling back to that night. She had argued with her father about the legislation, lost control of her shifting, fled to the forest… and Jared had followed her there. But he had never told her exactly *why* he was there in the first place. She looked up at him with wide eyes. "You stopped to come after me."

"I wanted to make sure you were safe," he rushed out. "That was all. And then… I…"

"You would have killed him," she said thickly, head buzzing. "If I hadn't decided to stop him and his anti-shifter legislation, you would have killed my father."

"No."

She whipped her gaze from the distant stare that had captured her back to his soft brown eyes. "No?"

He shook his head. "Once I met you, Grace… once I *loved* you… there was no way. It was you or him. I chose you."

"You chose me," she repeated in a whisper, her heart soaring.

"Yes." His eyes were wide, watching her like he was afraid she wouldn't understand.

Tears pricked her eyes. "So when you say *loved*… do you mean that hot, sexy thing we did in my bedroom? Or are you talking about love-love. The kind that, you know…" God, her words were tangling around her heart.

Something broke in his expression, and suddenly, his lips were on hers, his arms crushing her to him. It was hot and fierce and made her want to rip off the crisp jacket and shirt he was wearing right here, backstage. His mouth made demands of her that she willingly gave as her fingers dug into his shoulders, wanting even more. When he pulled back, they were both breathless.

"Love," he said, his breath hot on her lips, "as in I want to sink my teeth into you and claim you forever."

His words thrilled her, inside and out. Her wolf panted for more—to have him *now*—but instead she just nodded frantically.

"Yes," she gasped. "Yes, yes, yes." She pulled in a deep breath. "Wait… was there a question in there?"

He flashed a grin, then it tempered into a smoldering look that sent heat flushing to her lady parts. "Grace, will you be my mate?"

"Yes." No hesitation. She knew it meant forever. It was exactly what she wanted.

"Will you let me love you all the days of my life?" His dark eyes were swallowing her.

"Yes." She really wanted those lips back on hers.

He dipped his head, like he was going to kiss her, then stopped just short. "Grace Krepky, will you marry me?"

She gasped. But of course, that's what it meant. It was insane and wicked fast and... perfect.

"Yes," she breathed out.

His eyes blazed, and he drew her in for a kiss that held her captive, mind, heart, and soul... a kiss that she never wanted to end.

Chapter Seventeen

GRACE WAS SURE HER SCREAMS OF PLEASURE COULD be heard throughout the River family estate. But with Jared between her legs, performing sexy magic with his tongue and fingers, she couldn't bring herself to care. Or even think. Mostly, she was moaning his name and digging her fingers into his hair, urging him on.

"Oh, God, Jared, *please!*" He'd been teasing her so long, every muscle in her body was coiled tight in anticipation, waiting, begging for release.

He lifted his mouth from her sex and chuckled against the flat of her stomach while still slowly, tantalizingly thrusting two fingers inside her.

"Damn you!" She pulled her fingers from his hair and beat on his head instead.

Which only made him laugh more.

His thumb replaced his tongue in attending to her hyper-sensitive nub, making her gasp and arch her back—so close, but still not there—then he slid his deliciously hot body up the length of hers, pausing to give each of her tightly puckered nipples a taste before settling in at her neck. His thick and rock-hard cock pulsed heat into her side. She would happily have him use *that* on her, if he wasn't going to finish what he started with his mouth.

"You love when I tease you," he whispered against her neck.

"No, I don't, damn you." She bucked her hips against his hand, his fingers still far too slow in their rhythm. "Now make me come!"

"So demanding." But he was still laughing at her.

She was seriously going to make him pay for this.

It had been a week since she had announced her run for office—a week of tireless days of campaigning and pleasure-filled nights in Jared's bed, exploring every position, every tease, all the sex she never had in the years she was denying who, and what, she was. It was all one hazy dream, one climax after another, one triumph on the campaign trail following the next. Her life couldn't be more perfect, except… Jared had yet to claim her like he had promised. She didn't know what he was waiting for. With that, or with the slow torture between her legs.

She tried to wriggle away from his torments and turn the game back on him, but he held her fast. And truthfully, his massive, sexy body pinning her to the bed? His muscles rippling against her in his slow, rhythmic, seductive tease? His hot breath on her neck, panting his arousal, as if his massive cock probing her side weren't enough of a clue?

There was nowhere she'd rather be.

She turned her head to nuzzle into his ear. "If you don't hurry up, my love, I'm going to die from need."

He nipped at her neck. "If one could die from need, I would die every moment you're not right here underneath me."

And when he said things like that… her heart thrummed with more than just the breathy pleasure he was giving her. It filled to capacity with more love than she ever thought possible. *Especially* for her, the hidden shifter girl and Senator's daughter. Only now she was neither of those. She was out and proud and doing good things in the world with Jared by her side.

Or on top of her, as the case may be.

She threaded her fingers into his hair again, caressing his cheek with hers, matching his slow rhythm. "I want you, Jared River."

A low groan rumbled through his chest. His fingers thrust a little faster, his thumb striking lightning bolts of pleasure through her most sensitive parts. She slid one knee up along his arm, opening herself to him and touching him everywhere she could reach.

"I need you," she panted into his ear. "Every day. Forever."

His groan became a growl, and he slid his body down hers in a rush, diving back between her legs with his tongue. She let loose an animal sound that came straight from her wolf, but her claws stayed in, even though he was suddenly pumping her at a furious rate while lapping at her sex. She raced toward her climax, every muscle, inside and out, quivering toward the release.

Then she came so hard, she bucked up from the bed and curled over his head in her lap. He held her firm, working her through it, wrenching every last convulsion of pleasure out of her as her body squeezed down on his fingers. When the peak had washed over her, it left her completely limp.

She fell back on the bed, making it bounce. "You aren't a man," she said, still gasping. "Or a wolf. You're some kind of angel of pleasure. Or demon. I can't decide which."

He came up grinning. "I guess we'll have to keep experimenting… until you figure it out."

He slid up to kiss her full on the mouth, sharing the taste of her while pulling her body tight against him. Then his hand slid around from her back to cup her breast. He seemed to love playing with them, and she couldn't say no to anything that brought him pleasure. Not that she wanted to. His cock was pressing deliciously against her, reminding her that she wanted *that* next. Whether in her mouth or taking her in any number of positions, she didn't care.

But that wasn't exactly true. She *did* care. And maybe now was the time to ask.

When he broke from her mouth to focus on sliding slow kisses along her jaw, she forced herself to speak and not just lose herself in the sensation. "Jared."

He kept nibbling. "Ready to go again, my love? Because it's still early."

It was past midnight, but she wasn't complaining. "Jared, I need to know…" But then words failed her.

He froze mid-kiss then pulled away to look her in the eyes. "Need to know what?"

She searched his dark, concerned eyes. If there was something holding him back, something coming between them, she needed to know what it was. "Why haven't you claimed me?" she asked in a whisper.

He pulled back a little, the sexy glow on his face tempering. "It's not that I don't want to, Grace," he said carefully. "I hope that's not what you're thinking."

Actually, yeah, it was. She just shrugged.

He leaned in and kissed her so sweetly, it made her heart ache. "Every time I touch you, I want to throw you down on the bed and ravish your body. Sink my teeth in you and claim you, over and over."

Her breath hitched. *God, yes!* "So what's stopping you?"

He pulled back to look into her eyes again. "All of this has been so fast. So crazy. If you'll still have me, I'm going to marry you. But marriages can end. If you change your mind, there's always an out. A way to leave. Mating is forever, Grace."

She touched her fingertips to his lips, which were pressed tight with his concern for her. She really couldn't love this man any more than she did. Unless maybe the magic of the mating would allow it—she sincerely hoped so. She wanted to give everything to him.

"I know it's forever," she said softly. "That's why I want to do it."

"You've only known me for a little over a week."

She slid her fingers to hold his cheek. "I'm no expert on being a shifter, but from the very first moment, my wolf wanted you. She insisted on it. And when we made love, she simply knew—*you were our mate.* She knew it like she'd been waiting for you her whole life."

His concerned expression softened. "Oh, Grace." He seemed unable to say more.

"Isn't that how it's supposed to be?" she asked with wide eyes, concerned that maybe she had gotten this all wrong.

"No." He kissed her softly. "That's exactly how it's supposed to be."

"Then, dammit, Jared River, *take me.* Claim me. Give my wolf what she really wants."

He rumbled a growl in his chest again. "I was going to wait until after the wedding."

She reached down and stroked his cock, making him groan, which flushed fresh pleasure through her. "I don't want to wait. I want you now." She kept a firm hand riding up and down him, reveling in the silky-steel feel and the fact that his eyes had quickly hooded with pleasure.

"Are you sure?" His breathing was stepping up.

Would he really do it this time? "I couldn't be any more ready." These were the same words she'd already said to him, twice now for different things, and it was even more true today. Physically, emotionally, deep inside her wolf—she was ready in every way to become Jared River's mate.

He growled and yanked her hand away from his cock. She almost protested, but his large, strong hands quickly turned her over, propping her on her hands and knees. Then he thrust that gorgeous cock of his inside her. She shrieked with the suddenness of it, filling and stretching her with such complete- ness. He was so big that, even when he was gentle, it was still a shock to her system when he slid inside her. But now he was taking her hard and fast, growling and moaning, gripping her hips with his powerful hands as he thrust his enormous cock into her body—it was rougher than he'd ever taken her before, and she could hardly breathe with the pleasure of it.

"Is this what you want?" he growled as he pounded into her.

She could only whimper in response. Her climax was already building, rushing her entire body with the possession he was taking of it.

"You are mine, Grace. *Mine.* Always mine, just as I want you, just like this." His breath was heaving as much as hers, his voice harsh with power and dominance.

God, his words alone were enough to make her come... and they made her body quiver even more under the pounding. She braced herself to meet each thrust. The entire bed was shaking, and she was barely holding on, barely aware of anything but Jared's hands gripping her, his cock filling her... then her orgasm crashed and buried her like a wave, head to toe, her entire body fluttering. She cried out with it, her moan rising and falling with his thrusts working every pulse out of her.

Then he suddenly pulled out and stepped off the bed.

His cock was standing at attention, dripping wet with their lovemaking. His eyes were blazing, and his chest heaving.

"Submit to me, Grace," he demanded.

Jared wanted all of it—her submission, her love, her body writhing under his. His magic filling her blood. He wanted to fulfill every fantasy she had— but ravishing her just now had only brought out his alpha in a way that he hadn't felt in *so* long. She didn't merely bring him alive… she was making him whole.

And he would *have* her, dammit, the way he wanted her.

She belonged to him… and he wouldn't even exist without her.

She was his everything, and it was time he claimed her in the proper way.

"I… I don't know how to submit," she said, still on her hands and knees on the bed, her body flushed from the orgasm he'd just pounded into her. She was so damn sexy, her long, gorgeous hair mussed from their lovemaking and spilling every-where; that soft, innocent look on her wide sky-blue eyes goading him into ravishing her again.

"Come here on the floor with me." His voice was hoarse with need.

She skittered off, her thin body like a nymph doing his bidding. *Fuck*, his cock couldn't get any harder.

"Shift," he ordered. The submission pose would come naturally to her, once they were both in wolf form, but he didn't want to say that out loud. He wanted her to give it over to him, offer it up to him because her wolf was responding to his alpha. He wanted a true submission from her.

She obeyed his command, transforming into that beautiful, pure white wolf he had first seen dancing in the moonlight. He had wanted her then, but never thought in a million years it would be possible. He shifted as well, looming over her smaller wolf form, standing with his tail erect, ears perked, head held high—the alpha pose.

Submit to me. His thought command washed over her, and she nearly collapsed into the submission pose. The magic of her submission hit him like a thousand-watt blast. Her magic was *so strong.* And pure. And filled with such righteousness, he was cleansed by just being in its presence. It was unlike any other submission he'd experienced, even with his wife, Avery. Grace's magic made him more of an alpha, more of a man, than he had ever been before.

Rise, my love. His heart was overflowing with the magic of their bond... and this was only the submission. His mouth watered for the mating bond to come.

She leaped up from the submission pose and pranced a little, her tiny paws dancing on the floor —the submission bond was working its magic on her as well.

He shifted back to human. "Shift for me, Grace." He was panting with need for her.

The second she shifted, he grabbed her, turned her around and bent her over the edge of the bed. His hands were rough and demanding—because he knew it spiked her pleasure and because he couldn't hold himself back. He needed to be inside her, now, in every way.

With one hand holding her shoulder pinned to the bed and the other gripping her hip, he slammed into her. She gasped and moaned as he pounded her again, fast and hard, not holding back, giving everything he had. Possessing her body like he had wanted to from the start.

Her small cries of pleasure, the hard squeeze of her tight body around him, all of it was ramping him up so damn fast. He leaned over her, still thrusting, lifting his hand from her shoulder to swipe that long, gorgeous hair from her skin, clearing the way. His fangs came out, his mouth watered, and he bent to taste the sweet flesh of her neck, swiping his tongue across her to mark the spot where he would mark her. He could tell she was close again, her sweet flesh quivering around his cock as it drove into her. He hovered his fangs over her neck.

"You are *mine*, Grace," he whispered against her skin. "Forever mine."

Her sob of pleasure was too much for him.

He sunk his cock deep inside her at the same time his fangs pierced her skin. She cried out, convulsing under him, coming undone all around him. He clamped hard onto her neck, riding the waves with her, flushing his magic into her. His cock stiffened, and his own orgasm swept through him, shooting inside her and filling her with his seed. He held tight to her, pumping her full of himself, giving everything he had to her, claiming her forever. It lasted long, blissful, mind-blowing seconds.

When they both were finally coming down, he released her, then scooped her trembling body into his arms and carried her the rest of the way onto the bed. He held her like that, curled up in his lap, still shivering from her orgasm. He knew his magic was just beginning to course through her body—he could feel the bond tightening, pulling her closer to him, in a way only magic could. He touched her everywhere—with his hands and his lips and his soft words of love. She just shook and let out small moans as his magic permeated every cell of her body.

She was forever bound to him now. And him to her.

"Was it as good as you hoped?" he asked, knowing the answer, but wanting to hear it from her sweet lips.

"Holy fuck, Jared." She was still breathless.

He chuckled, and it shook the bed. He tightened his hold on her. "As fucks go, I think it's as close to holy as you can get."

"Please tell me we can do that more than once," she panted into the air, her head tipped back as he explored her neck.

"Again and again," he said with a grin against her skin. "Each bite just makes the bond stronger."

"I have never been so happy to be a wolf," she breathed.

He laughed, hard, and he could see the days stretching out in front of them. This amazing woman would give him more than he could possibly ever return.

But he was sure as hell going to try.

"Me too," he said, two short words from the depths of his soul.

Then kissed her again, like it was the very first time... and he hoped there would never be a last.

Chapter Eighteen

IT WAS WEDDING DAY, AND JARED WAS CONCERNED his mother might actually die from happiness overload. Not that he could blame her. All three of her sons were getting married. It was insane and awesome and, in his wildest dreams, he never thought something like this could happen. Especially for him.

Mama River was running around, ostensibly fine-tuning all the details, but she had done nothing for the last two weeks but set up things for this day. He didn't know what could possibly be left to do.

The wedding was at the River family estate, of course. The reception would be in the main house, which was already overloaded with white decor of every kind, from some kind of wispy fabric thing that traced a line throughout the house, to the twin-kling white lights hanging everywhere, to the heaping bouquets of white flowers perfuming the air. It was like a fairyland florist shop in there.

His mother seemed to think that *going overboard* wasn't possible when three sons were marrying at once.

The ceremony itself would take place out back, near the cabins that each of the brothers had remodeled for their new mates. All three of them had apartments in the city, but those seemed to be forgotten, at least for the moment. Jared heard Olivia had some kind of rat-trap apartment that Jaxson wouldn't even allow her to return to, except to gather up her things. Jace and Piper both had apartments in the city, but neither seemed in a hurry to leave the estate. There was lots of talk of nieces and nephews, and Jace had already outfitted their cabin with a small nursery tucked in the corner. Apparently, babies were on the agenda, and they were getting right on it. Which made Jared bust out with a smile. They might have little pups running around the family estate soon.

So much life. So much joy. His heart felt like it was bursting all the time now.

And for him and Grace, well, there was no

going back to her father's house, of course. Jared could move her into his tiny apartment in the city, but that didn't feel like home. And she'd never been around wolves or a pack, and there was so much he still wanted to show her, even outside the bedroom. The family estate just seemed like the right place to be.

Besides, Grace was so busy with the campaign —and would be for some time—that he was treasuring every second they had in their blissful little haven. Soon enough, she would be Washington's newest Representative to the House, and then she would be traveling all the time. His heart clenched, but he figured she would need a full-time bodyguard now, and there was no one else he would allow to have the job.

Jared strolled past the stables, heading toward the ceremony, and even here, Mama River had decked the place out. White papier-mâché wedding bells hung from the stable entrances, and bouquets of tiny white flowers were randomly tucked everywhere you might imagine. And some places you wouldn't. He passed the horses and the rows of cabins, finally arriving at the staging area where everyone had started to gather for the outdoor ceremony. There had to be over a hundred wolves in attendance, even though they were trying to keep it small. Nearly half that number actually lived at the estate right now—mostly the Wildings and the other wolves they had rescued. They were still hanging out, even though Agent Smith was dead, the Senator was shut down, and as far as they knew, his secret government program had been destroyed along with the hard drives. Or at least the parts of them that could be used for research. Grace had insisted that they preserve everything that showed what had happened—for history and for leverage against her father, in case he decided to cause problems for her. Or shifters in general. The Senator had slunk off after announcing he wasn't running for reelection, and as far as Jared knew, the man was hiding out in his Senate office in Washington DC, avoiding the press.

The wolves gathered for the wedding were milling around the seats—they were set up in rows on a giant white tarp his mother had acquired from somewhere. At the front was a white wooden arch decked out with more of that filmy white fabric, as well as dozens of white roses. The mountains rose in the background, and Seattle had decided to give them a perfectly clear blue-sky day in celebration. The soon-to-be brides were nowhere to be seen, but his brothers were gathered at the front, along with Owen, Jace's best man. Owen was Jace's brother-in-arms from Afghanistan and had been imprisoned by Agent Smith for over a year. Jared couldn't think of a better pick in that regard, either—Owen had been through hell and back, worse than any of them, and still came out of it with a smile on his face.

Jared hurried up to join them.

Jaxson and Jared were their own best men for the ceremony—Jaxson was his alpha, so that was obvious, and Jared had been the first to approve of Jaxson taking Olivia, a half-witch, for a mate. Anyone with eyes could see she was perfect for his brother... not to mention that she literally saved him. It was obvious to Jared that they belonged together, but it seemed important to Jaxson that Jared had been the first to state it out loud. His brother was alpha and anyone would have been honored to stand up for him. Jared thought maybe Olivia had a hand in Jaxson picking him.

He was happy he could do it with a whole heart.

"Are you ready to tie the knot?" Jared asked Jace, giving him a light punch on the shoulder.

Jace gave an incredulous look to Jaxson, who

was standing next to him. Owen was on the other side.

"I am seriously not used to that," Jace said with a smirk. "*Jared* with a smile on his face... it's really kind of freaking me out."

"Thanks a lot, bro." But Jared didn't take any offense. He knew the dark place he had come from, and that Grace had only barely saved him from it. There was nothing that could make him feel that way again, least of all a ribbing from his brother.

Jaxson grinned. "Judging by the sounds coming from Cabin Twelve, he's got a lot to smile about."

"Hey, now!" Jared complained. "Who had to listen to the both of you having fun with your new mates while I had none of my own?" He pointed to himself. "This guy. So you can all just deal with it."

Jace chuckled. "I don't know. You're setting a high bar over there. Piper wants more every time she hears Grace having too much fun."

"Sounds like a terrible problem for ya'll." Owen shook his head with mock sadness, his Texas twang coming out. "I'm just glad I'm staying in the main house. There's too much lovin' going on around here that's not in my bed."

Jace put his hand on Owen's shoulder. "Half

the female shifters here would line up for you, Owen, my friend."

"Only half?" Owen cocked an eyebrow. "I'm feeling an insult here."

Jace snorted. "Half should keep you busy enough. Why don't you take them up on it?"

"Cuz I respect your Mama, that's why." Owen gave him a horrified look that Jared wasn't quite sure was real.

Mama River was shuffling people into their seats, so Jared figured they must be getting started. He took up his position where his mother had instructed during the rehearsal and got an approving nod from her as she bustled about.

"Seriously, man," Jaxson said from his spot next to Jared. "I couldn't be happier for you and Grace. You've got a hell of a woman there, with what she's doing. And I think she's going to win."

"I don't doubt it for a second," Jared replied.

Jaxson nodded. "I like having you guys here at the estate, too. When she's ready, I'd like for her to join the pack. If that's what you both want." Jaxson gave him a questioning look, but he needn't worry. The last thing Jared wanted was to go off by himself, anywhere, again. Not if he could help it.

"I'll ask her," Jared said. "After the wedding. Maybe after a few more... honeymoons."

Jaxson just chuckled. Then a hush fell over the crowd, and their eyes were drawn forward, down the center row, to where the three brides were gliding in a slow and beautiful procession. Olivia, Jaxson's mate, wore a sweeping white gown that showed off her curves to maximum effect. Piper, Jace's mate, had a short snazzy number that was both outrageous and stunningly gorgeous. Jared smirked as his brother's eyes traced every curve. He didn't have to shift to know what Jace was thinking. Then, last in line, but first in Jared's heart, came his beautiful Grace. Her long, thin arms were bare, exposing the thin, crisscrossed scars she gained during her time with Agent Smith. His heart still clenched whenever he saw them, but he had stopped saying anything about them, especially to her. She wore them with pride—they were her initiation into the shifter world and her raison d'etre for running for office. If she could survive that, he had no doubt his lovely mate could do anything.

He tore his eyes away from her arms and focused on the rest of her. Grace's gown was simple —a pure white satin that hugged her slim curves and barely covered her perky little breasts straining underneath. Her long brown hair fell to her waist, and Jared couldn't help picturing her as Lady Godiva one more time. But that only made him want her naked and riding on top of him instead of a white horse.

The ceremony and the vows were simple—after all, they had already mated, already entwined their magic forever. The three brothers slipped rings on their new wives, making visible the human bond between them, but it could never be as strong as the magic that already bound them together. A justice of the peace Mama River had brought in from Seattle served to make it legal. When the short, scrawny man said, "You may kiss the brides!" the crowd let out a roar, the kind only wolves could make—half growl and half celebratory yowl.

Then it was back to the main house for champagne and an overwhelming amount of small plates that his mother had made and catered in for the affair. There was a lot of backslapping and cheek-kissing and general well-wishing.

Jared had never been happier in his life.

One of the Wilding cousins was setting up a DJ station, and Jared debated whether to stay for the full celebration, or haul his gorgeous bride back to their cabin for an early start on the honeymoon, but she was being mobbed by her admirers—she was already a celebrity in shifter circles for her act of bravery, coming out to the world as well as shutting down the Senator. Jared could stand to sit back and watch, let her have a moment in the sun before he squirreled her away all to himself. He was just joining Jace, Jaxson, and Owen for a drink when a commotion at the front door drew their attention.

Some kind of heated argument was going down at the door between a guest and some junior members of the Wilding pack who were serving as doormen.

"What's going on over there?" Jace asked with a frown.

"I don't know," Jared said, setting down his champagne glass. He peered around the throng in the great room blocking their view. "Isn't that Daniel Wilding at the door?"

Daniel had been captured by Agent Smith, like most of those in attendance, but only suffered a few of the tortures—but he had helped bring down the Colonel, his father, who had orchestrated the kidnapping and incarceration of several military wolves.

Including Owen, who spoke up first. "Yeah, that's him."

Jace craned his neck. "Piper invited her brother to the wedding, but he had some kind of appointment. Daniel said he would show up for the reception."

Owen frowned. "He's makin' quite a fuss."

"Yeah. I don't like it," Jace said.

Jared tipped his head, and his brothers and Owen followed him to the door.

"Is there a problem here?" Jaxson asked Daniel.

Daniel's red-faced anger didn't bode well for pretty much anything. "These idiots don't want me to bring bad news to your wedding," he said, tight-lipped. "And am sorry about that, but I figured you needed to know, regardless."

They were drawing the attention of the party-goers nearby. Mama River was making a sweep through the room, ensuring everyone had food and drinks, but having her three boys at the front door with tense looks grabbed hold of her attention. She started pushing her way through the crowd.

"All right," Jaxson said, grimly. "Out with it."

Daniel scowled. "Someone has doxed the entire Wilding pack."

"Doxed?" Owen asked with a dark look.

Jared gritted his teeth. "Doxing is when someone publishes your private information online.

Names, addresses. It's usually a revenge kind of thing."

"How the hell did they get hold of the Wilding pack private information?" Jaxson asked, eyes wide.

Daniel gave a pointed look to Jared. "Maybe the Senator had something to do with it."

Jared frowned. "He certainly has motivation, but how would he get hold of the Wilding pack information? You guys are scattered all over Seattle, not to mention the globe."

"It gets worse," Daniel said, his face drawing down further.

Mama River had worked her way through the crowd and come up to join them. "Worse in what way?" she asked.

"The information was released with some kind of YouTube video—guy in a mask reading off the Wilding pack and the River pack, outing them as wolves, giving all their detailed information. Some hate group, an anti-shifter group, is claiming responsibility for the video."

"*Fuck,*" Jace said, running a hand through his hair, glancing around the great room. "Do they know about the safehouse?"

"No," said Daniel with a fast shake of his head. "At least, it's not in the video."

Jaxson swore under his breath. "All right, no one leaves the safehouse. No one goes back to their normal homes. Not until we get this straightened out."

"Yeah, well, that might work for the River pack," Daniel said bitterly, "but as Jared said, the Wilding pack is spread all over. There's no way you'd have room for all of us, and besides, there's no way everyone's going to come hide out in the mountains. Including me."

Jaxson scowled in frustration, but Daniel was right.

"That's it," Mama River proclaimed. "I'm expanding the estate. Construction starts tomorrow. People can double up."

"That's great, Mama," Jace said, tightly, "but Daniel is right. Even if you have room, not everyone is going to come hide out here just because someone outed them as wolves. Especially the Wildings—trust me on this. Taking orders from others is not their strong suit."

"Then what are we going to do?" she demanded. "Because I'm not standing by while wolves get hurt."

That brought out nods from both of his brothers and Daniel, as well.

"It's simple," Jared said. "We take care of our own."

They might be separate packs, but if someone was outing wolves, especially a hate group... then they were all in this together.

Want more Shifters in Seattle?

Get the follow-on series to Riverwise Private Security…

WILD GAME (Wilding Pack Wolves 1)

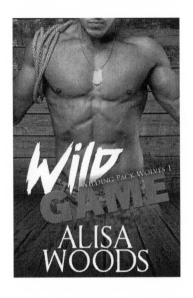

Owen's an ex-Army bodyguard for a beautiful gaming heiress… and a man with a secret.

Get WILD GAME today!

Subscribe to Alisa's newsletter

for new releases and giveaways

http://smarturl.it/AWsubscribeBARDS

About the Author

Alisa Woods lives in the Midwest with her husband and family, but her heart will always belong to the beaches and mountains where she grew up. She writes sexy paranormal romances about complicated men and the strong women who love them. Her books explore the struggles we all have, where we resist—and succumb to—our most tempting vices as well as our greatest desires. No matter the challenge, Alisa firmly believes that hearts can mend and love will triumph over all.

www.AlisaWoodsAuthor.com

Made in the USA
Monee, IL
24 March 2020